Five Fives

by
David Cunliffe

**Grosvenor House
Publishing Limited**

This book is published by
Grosvenor House Publishing Ltd
28-30 High Street, Guildford, Surrey, GU1 3EL.
www.grosvenorhousepublishing.co.uk

A CIP record for this book
is available from the British Library

ISBN 978-1-78148-344-2

Five months after the Millennium; location Tulsa, America. The radiant sun shone down in all its glory, a taxi cab moves steadily towards it's destination, the cab driver an old man clenching the steering wheel with his frail hands his bald head gleaming in the light of the midday sun. All of a sudden, he began blinking and frowning, seconds later he broke the anxious silence and spoke to his passenger.

"So son you said your name was Floyd, off to the Bland fifteen east fifth street".

Floyd gazed out of the window, not a bird on the wing or a cloud in the sky; he slightly opened the window and felt a cool breeze on his face. He then smiled condescendingly he was young, fresh-faced, fair-haired, he drew a deep breath and then replied, "One thing does puzzle me old man why is it called the Bland?"

Without hesitation the old man replied, "Son you don't know your history, Sue Bland was the name of the first oil well that's where all the money came from, it was completed in nineteen fifty it has fifty stories the height is five hundred and fifty feet".

Floyd smiled from ear to ear, "Cheers for that, you are a wealth of information. I must admit something else does spring to mind it's so quiet, no traffic, no people, the place is deserted apart from us.

"Well son in nineteen seventy-five the owner of the Bland paid out millions as he said it was as special day, twenty five years later and the new owner has done the same, the local people are well paid to simply disappear for the day".

"That my old friend is truly amazing. Oh you never gave me your name".

"It's Troy."

Floyd smiled, "Oh what an unusual name".

"Son, have you ever watched *Thunderbirds*?"

Floyd searched through his memory to when he was a child. "Yes I remember, were they the puppets that rescued other fellow puppets?"

"That's them son 'Thunderbirds are go'. Oh we're here, it's your stop". Troy hit the breaks and they both began to laugh out loud, "OK son everything's paid for. Cheers Floyd have a nice day".

Floyd slowly opens the cab door then steps onto the pavement; he closes the door behind him and then waves as the taxi pulls off. Floyd turns around and gazes up open mouthed at the magnificent structure, the Gothic architecture, statues of medieval saints and gargoyles all add to the overwhelming spectacle. All of a sudden, Floyd hears a deep gravelly voice.

"Good afternoon you must be Floyd the first of the five."

Floyd turned around there stood before him was an old man dressed all in black. Floyd looked at him steadily in the face, a gaunt looking man, hollow-eyed and with hollow cheeks, such a sinister sight, a walking, talking corpse. Floyd had a lively vivid imagination; he stood confused.

After a brief delay the old man said, "Your name is Floyd my name is Abbis I am the servant of Master Santo will you please follow me and I will take you to my meet him".

They both walk towards a set of double doors with engraved golden flames, the doors open automatically, with great hesitation Floyd enters after Abbis. Inside the spacious reception area, Floyd experiences a sudden feeling of wild amazement; statues of Roman and Greek gods, the ceiling and walls painted in vibrant colours, a marble stairway leading to the next floor, paintings hanging on every wall one in particular catches Floyd's eye.

"No it cannot be Leonardo da Vinci's *The Last Supper*, an amazing copy".

"No my friend this is the original, handed down through the generations, painted in the fifteenth century a gift to our creator David Burns".

Floyd looked confused, "Who was David Burns?"

"Much later my master will tell you all about him. I will now leave you with a thought, all of this could be yours and more, but for now take a seat and wait patiently for the other four to arrive". Floyd sat down and gazed up at the tall dark haired man complete with piecing raven coloured eyes, Floyd blinks.

The old man that stood before him disappeared into the shadows as the second taxi cab moves slowly towards its destination. The passenger looked out the cab window the radiant glory of the sun dazzling her beautiful blue eyes; casual dress the order of the day, the cab driver sits gazing into his rear view mirror intoxicated by her beauty.

"What did you say your name was again?"

"Oh it's Ilene".

"Nice name and your a nurse ain't you?"

"Yes I told you all of this when I first got in the cab," a look of disbelief on her face.

"Sorry Ilene its my age I am due to retire in five months, right we are getting close to the Bland now. I don't care much for the owner he calls himself Master Santo; some say he practices Devil worship. Don't trust him, be very careful my dear oh this is it, we're here."

The taxi stops and all of a sudden a knock on the window the cab driver looks up at Abbis, a look of fear on his face, his heart was pounding. Ilene opened the cab door and stepped out of the cab on to pavement. She then looked towards Abbis and shouted, "Who are you?"

"Oh I'm very sorry I startled you, my name is Abbis the servant of Master Santo".

"Its not me you startled it's the poor cab driver!"

"Well he does frighten easily, always asking questions and telling tales about my master I don't know why he even hired him".

Ilene closes the cab door and without hesitation the cab drives off.

"Ilene once again I can only humbly apologise for my rudeness; this way if you please." Abbis proceeds towards the entrance, closely followed by Ilene. The doors open, they enter and Ilene gazes all around and then she looks to the lonely figure sitting patiently. Floyd looks up at Ilene's angelic looks, her blue eyes and golden hair, such a comfort to the eye.

Floyd jumps to his feet, "Hi my name is Floyd".

"I know we have already met".

"No not you Abbis I meant the beautiful lady". His eyes turned full upon her.

"Oh I'll leave you both to get acquainted, take a seat next to Floyd".

Abbis then disappeared, Ilene laughs. "My that guy is sure strange!"

"My name is Ilene and you are Floyd". She drew closer and kissed Floyd on the cheek with her ruby red lips, her eyes glistened Floyd was bewitched by the leanness of her features, they sat down next to each other and began an in depth conversation.

A third taxi made its way towards The Bland, the cab driver a spellbinding lady looks to the passenger. "Hey cowboy I never caught your name".

"Its Vesta".

"What a name! Let me guess you're from Texas?"

"I sure am lady".

"Oh honey. Call me Belinda". Dressed in red satin, moisture shone all over her face, her long flowing raven coloured hair and emerald eyes left Vesta captivated.

"Belinda I must say its hard to believe your a cab driver your such an enchanting lady".

"Oh your such a flirt, I must say its not everyday I take such a handsome young man for a ride if you know what I mean".

"Yeah I've a very good idea".

"Vesta, we're nearly there, I've ran out of time".

"One more question?"

"What?"

"What do you do for a living back in Texas?"

"I am a rodeo rider".

"My god, cowboy any time you fancy a date look me up! Oh dam, this is the place".

All of a sudden the cab comes to a halt, she then turns around with a card in her hand, "There you go cowboy my card complete with contact numbers, I am living with my Aunt on the outskirts of Tulsa in an old converted church. Come an visit me but make sure you bring a bible and we can read it to each other, I could cook you a nice juicy steak".

Vesta looked at Belinda's teasing smile.

"Oh Vesta you know I am only joking I have such a wicked scene of humour".

Vesta smiles, then a knock on the window Belinda looks over her shoulder. "It's Abbis the master's servant, such a nice old man".

Vesta looks at Abbis. "My god he looks fresh from a Halloween party!"

Belinda opens the cab door. "Hi Abbis".

"Your beauty is as ever so radiant lady Belinda".

Vesta places the card in his pocket then opens the cab door. "Thank you beautiful Belinda I hope we meet again".

"Oh well I will have to love you and leave you my handsome prince".

Vesta laughs to himself. Belinda moves forward and then jumps out of the cab, she runs over to Vesta and kisses him tenderly on the cheek. Vesta then takes a deep breath the mysterious beauty smiles once more then proceeds back to her cab. With the blink of an eye she is on her way, waving with her left hand as she drives off.

Vesta waves back, Abbis looks to Vesta, "Don't worry sir I am quite sure your paths will cross again".

Vesta felt a sudden chill run up the back of his spine, he gazed into the menacing eyes of Abbis he hesitated then said, "What did you just say?"

"Oh Sir it doesn't matter take no notice of the ramblings of an old man, sometimes I don't know what I'm saying, this way!" The entrance doors opened and Vesta followed Abbis inside. "Look is it not magnificent sir."

Vesta smiled to himself in contentment then said, "Such priceless treasures, the paintings are the genuine?"

"Yes". Vesta turned his attention to the two fresh looking people sitting under the painting of *The Last Supper*. He then proceeded towards them introducing himself, Abbis disappeared in to the shadows. The fourth taxi cab drives towards the Bland.

Edris the fourth of the five speaks out! "Joe your taxi, I found the plates a little strange, Route 666."

"I know lady ain't they the beast, got them done five years ago who knows this cab could be taking you straight to hell." Joe was strange looking, extremely tanned, with heavily dark eyebrows and wispy grey hair. His particular laugh echoed around the cab.

"I know Joe your only joking".

"Hey lady it was you who said you were from Salem; whole lot of hell gone on there in the past."

"I know Joe my great great grandmother was accused of witchcraft!"

"Was she burnt at the stake?"

"No she died of fever".

All of a sudden Joe bursts out in song, "Oh what a nice way to burn, fever I am on fire fever burning through the night. I got the fever".

"My god you're singing".

"Sorry lady I'm a big Elvis fan!"

Edris laughs, she had short brown hair with an athletic build.

"Hey lady the year is two thousand, all that talk about the world ending I believe it will end when it's good and proper".

"You reckon Joe?"

"I sure do lady! And here we are," Joe hits the breaks and the cab grinds to a halt, and then turns to Edris. "It's been nice knowing yeh lady".

Edris looks in to his hollow eyes with a puzzled face. "What ever do you mean?"

"Oh I just mean have a nice day".

"Ok Joe thanks".

Edris opens the cab door and then closes it behind her, Joe laughs waves and pulls off. Edris turns, in front of her is a particular looking old man.

"Hi Edris you are the fourth to arrive, the rest are waiting, my name is Abbis I am very pleased to meet you. This way my dear". Edris follows him through the doors into the building "Look over here the others are dying to meet you, go on introduce yourself! Don't be shy, they won't bite".

Edris hurries towards them, thinking at least they look normal whilst Abbis once again melts in to the shadows.

"Hi you all, my names Edris". She shakes hands with Vesta. "My you sure have a strong grip!"

"Sorry I'm a rodeo rider back in Texas".

"What do you do for a living Edris?"

"I am a tarot reader and seer".

"You mean you can see into the future?"

"Well sometimes if the price is right".

"OK here is a challenge for you, at present there are two males and two females describe the fifth person before they arrive".

Edris closes her eyes for a brief second. "I have a mental picture of the final person, a tall dark handsome male over six foot, a real fighter."

Edris then introduces herself to the others. The final taxi cab makes its way towards The Bland the cab driver speaks. "Hey son if you don' mind me asking where did you get that black eye from, are you a boxer? The reason I'm asking is cause I used to box in the late sixties I was called the Cobra".

"Yes I am a boxer".

"I thought I recognised you, Rocky Steve Ransom."

"That's right".

"God you were sure unlucky in your last fight, five round stoppage, you didn't see that left hook. My whole life has been devoted to boxing I watch as many fights as I can you have had five professional fights, four wins and one loss is that right?"

"No it was the left". They both break out in laughter; all of a sudden the taxi cab pulls over. "This is it The Bland, hope you put on a good show Rocky!"

"I'll try my best "

"Hey in the sixties I was a big big snake".

"I bet you were".

They both start laughing again Steve then opens the taxi cab door climbs out and closes it behind him whilst spontaneously waving as the cab drove away. Steve then turns around there standing behind him is Abbis.

"Hi, you must be Steve! My you are such a big fellow I am the servant of Master Santo now please follow me."

They both enter the building Steve looks around mesmerised by the glorious surroundings as Edris awaits a close view of the newest addition. Steve looks over at Edris smiling, "Tall, dark and handsome".

Steve walks over to her, they all look to one another in amazement. "Hi I am Steve".

"Hello Steve I am Edris, this is Vesta, Floyd and the stunning Ilene, Steve I am a tarot reader and seer". Vesta challenged me to predict your gender, looks and height, I said you would be a male, tall dark and handsome.

"Cheers Edris that's me all over".

"And I said you were a real fighter".

"That's also correct I have been boxing for fifteen years, the name is Rocky Steve Ransom."

"Yeah I can tell by the shiner". Steve laughs then Abbis appears.

"Right everybody your attention please, listen to what I am about to tell you, each of you will compete for the ultimate prize. Property and wealth worth five billion dollars. It will be all yours to do with what you like, each of you flew from your birth places to Tulsa on a private jet. You all stayed in different five-star hotels my Master must retire he has served us well, you are all twenty-five years of age, healthy and intelligent. I can tell by each of your eyes you like what I am saying, now its time to meet my Master. All of you follow me he awaits our company on the fifth floor".

"Hey Edris did I hear him right, five billion dollars?" Vesta looked to Edris with a look of disbelief on his face. Edris nodded in confirmation her emerald eyes began to sparkle with pure delight as they all follow Abbis to the lift he presses the button, the doors open and then they all enter their faces glowing with anticipation. The doors then close and once again Abbis presses the button that takes them all to the fifth floor.

They soon arrive at the fifth floor and with a slow and solemn movement Abbis opens the doors. Floyd takes hold of Ilene's hand, "this is it soon very soon I'll be rich".

Ilene starts to laugh; Abbis then lost his usual composure, no laughing trying hard to control his anger with an edge of coldness he spoke as they all stood motionless and listened.

"This is your hour; only one of you can win, concentrate the minute each of you step into the room will become an individual, remember silence, no laughing".

Floyd released Ilene's hand, his face horror struck. "This way all of you this way".

He had such firmness in his voice as he moved abruptly and caught his breath. They all walked to the end of the corridor, it was decorated with medieval tapestries and they arrived at a door engraved with 'Five Fives'. The door opened as if by magic, Abbis entered and the five followed. Once inside they all gazed around mesmerised by the priceless treasures. It was an enormous room glaringly illuminated. Steve looked to the high ceiling painted in a similar style to the Sistine chapel. All of a sudden, a large tall dark-haired man appeared dressed all in black, just like his servant Abbis. The features on his face were hard to read.

They all stood still and watched with fixed fascination. He then spoke with a loud dominating voice, a face of cool ivory. A born leader.

"Right I want you all to relax, my name is Santo. I know all of your names Floyd, Ilene, Vesta, Edris and last but not least Steve. I want to thank all of you for coming, you are the chosen one's. I would now like to show you the priceless treasures. All of this will be yours if destiny takes a shine to you. Right over there a marble statue of David sculptured by Michelangelo in the fifteenth century, he also completed this beautiful painting; The separation of Light from Darkness.

"All follow me to look at another Michelangelo masterpiece, The Creation of the Sun and the Moon, remember be open minded; are they all fake or original?"

Edris points to a picture, "Look it can't be, is that the Mona Lisa".

"Yes it can, this is the original the other is a fake."

Steve stands next to a small replica of the Santo Maria made from gold and precious gems; the fine detail was amazing, the gems sparkled, a treasure to the eye.

"Is it not remarkable that in the late fifteenth century Christopher Columbus sailed across the sea and discovered our great nation? Right my friends over to the left is a round table with six can you all sit on the seat that has your name engraved on it".

Five golden seats and a large oak table decorated with golden tears. They all walk over to the chairs and sit down. All of a sudden Abbis appears with a pyramid shaped object, he handed it to Santo who was sitting at the head of the table. The pyramid was decorated with Egyptian letters, in the centre a large eye, he places his hands on either side of the pyramid, it then opens and he then produces five stacks of cards and placed them on the table. With slight hesitation he lifts out a strange looking object.

"Behold the eye of Cavoc, you will all slip into a trance, then you will take a journey to the fifteenth century, I see you are all glowing with anticipation at this stage, I ask you to al remain calm and above all relaxed".

All of a sudden the lights faded, Santo placed the eye of Cavoc around his neck and then he started to speak in a strange language, his words radiated a deep sense of peace. Instantaneously they all slipped into a trance like state.

"I shall now begin in the sixteenth century Tudor times, Henry VIII was king, after him we had bloody Mary and then my favourite Elizabeth. The start of the golden age, we had Galileo Galilel the father of modern science Michelangelo and Leonardo da Vinci, later we had the greatest writer of all time, William

Shakespeare. Our great master David Burns visited Nostradamus, he assisted him on his journeys they both believed life is but a series of numbers that govern our destiny or demise.

"David studied the Wicca which states the universe is made up of five classic elements, water, earth, air, fire and ether. Human beings and other primates have five digits on each hand as well as five toes on each foot, according to some traditions of Maya Mythology we are now living in the fifth world. I will now begin telling the story of David Burns he was born in Flint, a Borough sea port and Parish in the poor-law Union of Holywell in the year fifteen hundred.

"These were Tudor times, a Welsh English family that ruled England from 1485 until 1603. England was a farming society ninety percent of the population lived in small villages and made a living from farming.

Since the fourteenth century poor harvests resulted in localized starvation and a high mortality rate, it was a time of decay people bathed but only once a year on the fifth month. The population of Flint was static for many years, and then the great Plague spread from China into Asia and across Europe then England. The black death had arrived, it was so called because the skin of the affected became intensely dark and death followed within a few hours. Henry VII became King of England after the battle of Bosworth

"A brief history lesson now on to the story of David Burns. His mother, Abbey of Welsh origin, his father

Blake was English. Both his parents were born in 1490. They all lived on the outskirts of the village, in a dwelling made of wood with a thatched roof surrounded by elms and sycamore trees, this was a poor Tudor house, wooden shutters and beds with mattresses filled with straw."

David now eight years of age, a young man sits on a small wooden chair, fresh faced with a pale complexion lost in a world of his own patiently awaiting his main meal of the day. Hunger soon gets the better of him. "Mum is it nearly ready?" His mother was a delicate looking woman, her face always extremely pale. "David it's nearly ready". He watched as she stirred the broth with fixed fascination.

"Your father should be home soon with your sister Carol". As soon as she finished her sentence the door opened it was Blake and Carol.

"Hi Abbey something smells nice."

"Come and take a seat my husband, did you get the barley and rye?"

"Yes I have them here," he places two bags onto the table.

"Carol my dear what is that you've got?"

"Oh mum it's fresh bread".

They all sit down ready to eat; Blake places the coarse grey bread onto a plate then to carve through it with a sharpened knife. David's father was of medium height; he had ice blue eyes and light brown hair he had been educated by his father who was a very wise man. His wife Abbey always puts on a brave face, but she constantly worries about the future of the family, very soon the broth was all gone.

"My that broth was tasty," said Blake smiling.

Abbey was looking in to Blake's eyes and summoned up the courage to speak, "Blake I've been thinking how about you working in the old mines, I believe they pay really well."

Blake tried hard to control his anger, "Look Abbey I am not going to work in no dark pit for any amount of money."

He had an angry expression written all over his face, a moody and dogged silence fell about the place as Blake took a deep breath, then glazed in to Abbey's eyes.

"Look Abbey I have told you before I made enough money for us to survive fighting as an archer in the battle of Bosworth, my father God rest his soul fought in France as an archer. He fought the maid of Orleans.

"I shall not work in any mine, my skill is with the bow as was my fathers, our daughter Carol is well educated I paid for it, she travelled to Dover and now she is betrothed to the local magistrate. Next month she is to be married making herself a better life".

Abbey smiles, "I am sorry, you are right, you have always been a good man. We have goats, chickens and pigs, and a horse; it seams as ever I just over worry about nothing. Come over here my husband let us embrace."

Blake walks across the room; Abbey's eyes begin to glisten with tears as they hug each other. The radiant glory of the sun shines through the window of their humble home. David stands up and wanders past his preoccupied parents his sister follows him, David opens the door then leaves. Carol follows in hot pursuit, they both walk outside Carol soon catches up with him.

"David do you want to feed the animals with me?" David remembers the strong smell of the pigs.

"No thank you I'll go for a walk up to the cross roads and get me some fresh air."

"Oh little David do be careful."

"I know you say it every time watch out for witch Hazel she lives up that way and she could turn me in to a toad."

His sister stood insanely laughing. David turned and hurried away pretending not to be frightened. The summer was glorious, David walked alone, lost in his own world. He stopped suddenly and glanced down by his feet, an odd stick of wood caught his eye; he picked it up and pretended it was a magical sword striking it against the hedgerows.

"I am not afraid of any old witch".

All of a sudden a draught of cold air, a sudden chill ran down his spine. He had ventured close to the crossroads near the old cottage, the dwelling of hazel the old witch. David sensed someone standing behind him, fearfully he turned around slowly a look of disbelief on his face he shivered through his frame it was Hazel the witch, in the flesh standing before him. He stood motionless her death-cold, dark piecing eyes flickered on her malignant face. Dressed all in black an evil smile on her cruel wrinkled mouth, she cackles then speaks with an edge of coldness.

"Don't be afraid young boy I only want to talk to you".

David summoned up the courage to reply. "Why do you want to talk to me?" he gazed fearfully.

"You are a special little boy the voices have spoken to me, enlightenment is the key to your destiny".

David looked up at the witch confused, he then gathered up the courage to speak again, "What voices?"

"Oh so sweet, so innocent, it is good you question me I like that".

"I will be gone in five moons, eventually you will meet the maker Cavoc and he will fulfil your destiny."

David stood paralysed with fear awaiting the witch's next move, she smiled showing her decayed brown and yellow teeth, her eyes wide, she was pure evil. All of a sudden she shrugged her shoulders and hurried past David towards her domain. David doesn't hang around and ran all the way home dropping his magic sword on the way. He looks to his parents standing hand-in hand in the doorway of their dwelling David ran over to them his face flinching a shade of terror.

Abbey stepped forward and got hold of her son. "What's the matter son?"

"Mum it's the witch she spoke to me."

"David you didn't go near the crossroads what have you been told"?

David's heart raced shaking with fear.

"Calm down. Calm down, what did she say?"

"She said voices had told her I will meet Cavoc in the future".

Blake shakes his head.

"Frightening innocent young children, I will go and see her."

Abbey stared at Blake wide-eyed. "No I have heard other folk talk, they have been gathering word on her she has cursed many."

"Not you Blake I don't want you going anywhere near her."

"Alright I won't Abbey."

David looks up at his father slowly regaining composure".

"Come here son".

David embraces his father, "The stories of your brave father fighting in France, can you tell me some stories?"

Abbey smiles, "Go on Blake take him inside and tell him some stories, I know that will cheer him up."

Blake takes a deep breath, "Come on then son, wipe away those naughty tears from your eyes. I'll have no weeping when I tell you stories of bravery."

David takes his father's hand and then walks inside and they both sit beside the open fire, Blake closed his eyes for a brief second then smiled.

"Right I'll begin this is the true story of my father Casey".

David nodded glowing with anticipation he loved the genius and intellect of his fathers stories.

"My father Casey was born in fourteen hundred and ten, he was a first class archer and he could fire fifteen arrows per minute, the English long bow was used in the battle of Agincourt. A famous victory in which five thousand archer's under the vision of King Henry V, defeated a French army five times it's size. The French lost ten thousand men, the English lost five hundred, my father also told me about the victories at Crecy and Poitiers.

Casey was trained at a very early age, he competed in tournaments that were held on a regular basis and he was picked out and recruited for military duty into an elite group of archers. He could hit a target at four hundred yards his weapon was developed from the Welsh longbow that had been used against the English in the twelfth century. In fourteen twenty-five, his wish was granted; a journey to France to do a battle for a famous Earl who had heard about Casey's archery skills and visited him when he was in Calais.

He introduced himself then told Casey all about Orleans, he was tall; his skin was discoloured with a dark beard and pointed nose. His voice was very deep. "Casey you and your fellow archers are to accompany me to Orleans".

Casey gazed into Edgar's raven coloured eyes. "Sir how do you know so much about me?"

"Well Casey your trainer was a relation of mine, uncle James he trained you how to use the longbow".

Memories came flooding back, "Yes I remember James, a tall man, with a white beard and a pale complexion, always smiling".

"Yes that's him".

"He told me you are one of the best archers in England, if you ever had need of anything then let me know."

"We shall be friends," Casey nodded slowly,

"Just remember one thing, the French have a gut hatred for the English, always watch your back".

"Right let us be on our way".

Edgar walked to his horse, his armour shone in the bright sunlight, as he mounted his raven coloured horse. David joined his fellow archers and they all mounted their horses and soon they were all on their way. Casey gazed up at the driving clouds the forest all around cried out before the wind. The endless march continued, thunder rumbled in the distance, masses of dark clouds arrived and the landscape became dark. They rode to the light of the moon Casey was mesmerised by the shadows all around him. Faster and faster the horses galloped soon they all rode from the dark forest and James felt relief as in the distance was Orleans. Crossing a field of mud a feeling of relief entered the hearts and minds of the weary men. It was now sunset the drawbridge opened and the men entered the fort. Casey could here the distant cries of reinforcements. Casey looked all around Orleans; a large walled city, one of the most fortified in France, all of a sudden silence engulfed the Fort.

The French inhabitants all around visibly flinched, an old man grinned at Casey, his teeth black and yellow his face old and haggard, and then the sound of French trumpets echoed all around, Edgar suddenly appeared. "Casey you and the other archers get up to the ramparts," the fort was defended by five thousand men. Casey stood on the Northern ramparts and he could see in the distance a mass of bright colours, gold, red, silver and blue the flags of the French army, the army consisted of ten thousand men.

The siege machines appeared before his eyes, five monstrous catapults, Casey gazed open mouthed at the size of the French army, he then turned his head to the right he saw a knight mounted on a fine warhorse, covered in armour from head to foot. In his hand a white banner embroidered with white lilies, Casey was transfixed by this mysterious knight; he watched as the brave knight rode around the besieged city walls. The astonished English soldiers started cheering and laughing at the sight of this small knight.

Edgar approached Casey, "My friend you look puzzled."

"Who is it Edgar?"

"My men recognise her its Joan the cowgirl, that is why all the men are laughing and cheering, no French cowgirl is going to take Orleans".

Suddenly Joan rode off in a different direction.

"Casey ready yourself; soon the French will attack". Casey reached for an arrow from his white linen bag, the French fired the catapults. Heavy bolts whistled overhead like flashes of lightning. The French trumpets sounded, Casey felt his mouth go dry, reflecting a shade of terror as the French advanced on foot, their armour gleaming in the midday sun. Casey leaned on the ramparts and strung an arrow in his bow. He watched as the French lifted their siege ladders it was time Casey let flight an arrow, and then another. Casey turned his attention to the screams of the dying and the clash of steel, the noise rose and rose.

Siege ladders were erected all around the city walls, Casey watched in horror as an English knight beat a French solider across the head with a giant mace. The fighting became more and more intense and continued all day. Silence then became the order of the day as a truce was enforced to remove the dead. The field reeked of death, mud and blood. Casey relaxed, he took a sip of water and ate some soft bread, Edgar appeared and he spoke almost breathlessly with fatigue.

"Casey the Duke has informed me a peasant girl slipped through our defences entered the City and told the people of her visions, she said she was on a mission to rid France of us, what makes things worse is she has aroused the people and the French army with courage and faith".

"Oh god what are we to do, they well out number us tomorrow?"

"They will attack again. I wonder could you Casey preform a small miracle, you will be well rewarded for your efforts, I want you to call upon your archery skills I want you to shoot an arrow and put an end to this false prophet".

A peculiar shiver ran down Casey's spine as he gazed fearfully at Edgar's grin of malice with an edge of coldness he spoke, "Rest for now but ready yourself for the next attack then you will do my bidding".

Casey nodded and then sat frozen motionless he could not rest until the job was done he slowly stood up and turned his attention to the French tents and colourful banners moving to and throw, alive with the cry of the wind.

High above their tents the light started to fade, Casey looked up as the stars shone brightly, he then lay down closed his eyes and dreamt of the task ahead of him. Daybreak soon followed, the sunlight was bright and warm the familiar sound of the French trumpets echoed in Casey's ears as he jumped to his feet and then shaded his eyes for a brief second as the sun in all its glory shone down on Casey.

A loud deep and gravely voice shouted, "They are attacking again". Casey gazed over the ramparts the French cheered; it was Joan she had roused the fighting spirits that had lain dormant for so long. It was the fifth of May, a French archer fired an arrow over the ramparts landing inside the Fort carrying another message asking the English to abandon France and return to England or face the wrath of God. Casey learned over and picked up his bow the French attacked and the sound of battle, mid morning madness rose to the sky.

Casey had only one target in his sight, Joan directing the soldiers with great spirit. Casey aimed; Joan sat on her horse waving her sword as she raised her visor. Casey looked down, his imagination playing tricks on his mind. The eyes of an angel looked his way; Casey hesitated for a brief second. He then fired the arrow like a bolt of lightning, the arrow hit Joan just above her breastplate she looked up at Casey then fell forward as the French knights raced forward to give her protection.

Edgar appeared on the rampart. "Casey you hit her!"

The Earl waved a defiant fist at the French knights as they retreated, guiding Joan to safety the army followed. Edgar embraced Casey and cries of relief followed his every move.

"Casey you shall be rewarded".

The death cold eyes of Edgar made Casey have strong shudder. "Come with me Casey you shall have your reward"

Casey followed the Earl past the ever-grateful soldiers. They climbed down the steps.

"Casey this way!"

They entered a room full of stolen French bounty.

"Casey I want you to have this small chest it was taken off a French baron; here take it".

Casey picked up the chest and he then placed it on to an old oak table.

"Look inside".

Casey, glowing with anticipation opened the chest inside was fifty pieces of silver, a pack of tarot cards and a pack of playing cards.

"What do you think say something?"

"I don't know what to say, but Edgar what if she is only wounded?"

"If that is the case then you will give me back twenty five pieces of silver, as you have not completed your task. Am I being fair Casey?"

"Yes Edgar what you say is fair."

"Casey you are right to think she may recover, if she is indeed a witch a spell could bring her back to lead the French".

All of a sudden a knock on the door, it opens and standing before them a dark eyed face reflecting a shade of terror, "Sir the witch, she's back, the French are attacking again".

The Earls face, was a mask of fear. "I saw the arrow piece above the breast plate, yet she leads her army into battle. Casey you tried your best, keep all the silver, eventually we will get her do not concern yourself my friend. Quick now to the ramparts".

Casey and the Earl hurried to the ramparts the usual cries and the clash of steel echoed all around. Casey and the Earl looked over the ramparts and witnessed Joan ride her horse swiftly to the fort and touch it with her banner the French fought with such ferocity. The battle continued until nightfall and then the French retreated. The Earl spoke to his men, "We must retreat, leave the fort before the next attack, we must leave now. Collect all your belongings let us be on our way". The English left before dawn. The French soldiers were jubilant at the victory and called Joan the Maid of Orleans; by this name a legend was born. Casey stayed in northern France and he learnt how to read the tarot cards and lived off the silver the Earl had given him.

Casey was sat in a room thinking back to the battle of Orleans when all of a sudden the Earl knocks then enters the room, Casey stood up.

"Casey I am here to tell you we are to join the Duke of Burgundy, tomorrow we ride to reinforce his army. This Joan has won several victories against us and she has helped Charles to become King, she was at his Coronation in Rheims, this is why we are here stuck in northern France we have been driven here by a peasant girl.

"Casey are you alright you seem withdrawn since you fired the arrow into Joan it is not your fault she is still alive? Casey come outside let us talk some more."

Casey looked at the Earl, the features of his face were hard to read. They both walked outside the atmosphere was cold with a disagreeable damp smell. The Earl walked with Casey and all of a sudden a soldier shouts; "Riders approaching, riders approaching". Casey and the Earl turned and saw three knights entering the fortification they stopped and then dismounted from their horses. The first knight walked over to the Earl. "I have an important message from the Duke, the peasant girl known as Joan has been captured she has been delivered to the prison in Rouen". The Earls face showed a cruel smile.

"Good I knew it was but a matter of time, how was she caught?"

"She rode a large grey steed with a cloth of gold over her breast plate, she and her knights attacked the City she was the most valiant member of the flock. They attacked and attacked we outflanked them. They were well out numbered and an archer by the name of Rodger grabbed hold of her pulling her from her horse, she tried to remount and was then taken prisoner".

The Earl looked at the knight, "I want you to take me and my friend to Rouen do you understand?"

The knight gazed into the Earls cold eyes he knew he had to obey. "Yes earl I will take you there".

"Good get yourself some food and water whilst we ready ourselves". The Earl the turned to Casey. "I want to see this peasant girl suffer, I remember Orleans. I must banish these demons; defeated by a peasant girl". The Earl was constantly haunted by the defeat. Casey stared into his bitter cold eyes with his usual composure and he agreed to the mission. Casey collected his belongings he the Earl and the three knights mounted their horses and rode onto Rouen prison. With great haste they soon arrived, Casey could hear a thunderstorm rumbling in the distance Rouen prison was dark surrounded by a dark landscape.

The light faded rapidly Casey was shown to his room and got into bed, a storm raged fiercely throughout the night. Casey closed his eyes and faded into a deep sleep and an angel appeared to him in his dreams. She told him he had a good heart born into a cold world, she told him her name was Mary. She explained, "Very soon you will find the solitude and peace you so desire". She told him he would have a son who marries and in turn have a son who will be very special, the angel had blue eyes and golden hair, and her features were truly heavenly."

Casey awoke with a feeling of enlightenment, he moved swiftly without noise, he drank some water and then got dressed. He opened the door as the Earl approached him.

"I have bad news my friend I am called away, you must stay and be my eyes and ears, you will watch the witch burn. I have spoken with the Duke he has informed me she will confess and soon she will burn". Casey gazed at his cruel face and then a grin of malice. His cold weary voice sent a strong shudder through Casey's soul.

"If you need anything Carte is your man, I have told him to see to your every need and he has been informed you are to be one of her guards". Casey was lost for words and just nodded, the Earl then left with great haste. Casey felt relieved, peace at last. He then visited Joan; the jailer opened the cell door and before Casey sat a young woman fitted with leg irons.

Casey's heart was pounding, he gazed into her eyes mesmerised by a glimmer of light that surrounded her features, his eyes were turned full upon her he was mesmerised by her transcendental beauty.

"I am sorry I wanted to say something to you, it was me who fired the arrow in Orleans. I remember it hit you above the breastplate I have heard people say that you hear voices. I too hear voices. I have spoke to an angel her name was Mary."

Joan looks into Casey's eyes, "You are a good man I knew you would come, Mary has also spoke to me, and she said we are from the same blood line. Casey I forgive you, leave France and seek out the peace and solitude you so desire".

"You are no witch you are but a messenger from God listen hide your thoughts, if anyone suspected you have heard the same voices as me you would share the same fate. You said we shared the same blood line." Casey was glowing with anticipation of the awaiting answer Joan smiled in a low voice she said.

"I will die, you will leave France never to return and the blood line will be intact this is all I can say now, you must leave the guards are approaching."

They smiled at each other then the door to the cell opened. "Casey you must leave now its time for her trail."

Casey turned recovering from his enlightenment, completely at peace with his soul. Joan stood trial, she was charged with sorcery and heresy. She told her judges, "God has always been my guide in all that I have done."

Joan was told on the fifth month of the year she was to be burnt at the stake for heresy and witchcraft. In the market place at Rouen soldiers brought forward faggots. Casey walked over to Carte and asked whether he could see the prisoner before she died?

"Has she put an evil spell on you Casey, why on earth would any English man want to see her? Casey you will see her soon burnt at the stake".

Casey looked upon him with pity, a rough spiteful man, death cold eyes such a sinister sight. Casey turned away knowing he was surrounded by good and evil. He walked over to the main square where a crowd of people had assembled in anticipation of Joan's demise. All of a sudden Joan appears escorted by guards ushering her towards the stake of death, they fastened her to the stake then surrounded her with faggots. Casey moved closer he had made a crude cross out of an old stick a voice had told him to be brave and hand Joan the crudely made cross, a priest read out loud to Joan she caught sight of Casey in the crowd. He knew what she wanted as he moved forward and reached over to Joan and handed her the cross. Joan smiled and thanked Casey she then tightly held the cross to close to her bosom.

The priest read out another prayer Casey gazed at her open-mouthed. Joan then kissed the cross as the guards lit the fire. They were cruel flames, only her legs burnt; anger and sorrow engulfed the heart of Casey. The duration of her agony has over half an hour the flames rose and she cried out Jesus five times. Soldiers and civilians were falling to their feet in tears of pity. Casey felt his mouth go dry, he covered his head in shame and began to weep uncontrollably at the sickening sight he had just witnessed. Casey fell to his feet and prayed for Joan's soul how could man be so cruel. All of a sudden Casey heard laughter he stood and watched in disbelief as the executioner picked up from the ashes Joan's intact heart then preceded to the river Seine where he cold-heartedly threw the heart into the cold water. Casey then shouted in disbelief. The guards and the executioner watched Casey with fixed fascination and he knew it was time to leave and return to England.

Casey gathered his belongings, mounted a horse and left forthwith, he knew the Earl would come after him when he found out he had deserted; he returned to

Essex. He told is friends all about his ordeal he then turned to religion and moved to North Wales to escape the bitter memories of the cruel war. His new home was in Flint. The Earl died shortly after Casey had deserted France in a hunting accident, my father was haunted by the sight of Joan's death.

He would often gaze into the fire; he would stare and lose himself amongst the flames. He told me he had witnessed an angel burnt at the stake, he died of a broken heart in fourteen seventy-five. I was five years of age my mother Susan looked after me until she died in fourteen eighty-eight. I then met your mother Abbey the rest is history. David looked up at his father growing drowsy the story seemed to go on forever. He smiled then all of a sudden the door opened it was Abbey.

"You finished your story yet Blake?"

"Only just, I was telling David the story my father used to tell me about Joan of Arc. I bet one day you would like to visit France just like your Grandad did".

"Yes France and Italy."

Abbey and Blake laugh as the door suddenly opens, it's Carol she enters the room then pulls up a chair and sits down.

"Here she is my little princess bright and beautiful that's what you need David education, just like your sister. She can speak Latin and read and write. Have you received word from Edwin?"

"Yes father he wants me to move to Dover to be his Bride."

"What do you think Abbey? We have met Edwin, he is a good-hearted man and he also has wealth and property. I believe you're destined to be together forever. When does he want you to move to Dover then?"

"I read his letter, I don't know how to put this' tomorrow evening."

"That is soon I must admit. I wasn't expecting it to be that soon."

"Is it alright father?"

"Of course it is!" He looked into her eyes and knew this was the right thing to do.

"Edwin is sending a carriage to pick me up".

"That is settled then, we all need to get some sleep".

Darkness fell all around; the only light was a candle slowly burning on an old oak table. They all climb into their beds and fell into a deep sleep, David opens his eyes and watches the candle flicker and then a party of field mice scurried along the table breaking the silence of the night. David remembered the story his father had told him it played on his mind as he fell asleep, he dreamt of the maid of Orleans as she spoke to him in his dream.

"David are you a saint or a sinner?" Her angelic eyes shinning like golden crystals. I don't claim to be either, my grandfather's heart melted at the sight of you burning at the stake.

"Yes sweet boy, this is true. I forgave him he had no part in my execution. When you are a lot older you will feel as I did until that day, you will seek answers the pathway to power awaits you in France".

Joan slowly disappears from David's strange dream, her voice echoed all around the dwelling. David and his family start to open their eyes to the dawning of the new day.

Blake opens the door and then proceeds to fetch some water. The radiant glory of the sun shone onto David's bed he rubbed his eyes then climbed out of bed.

"Did you have a nice sleep David?"

"Yes I dreamt of the maid of Orleans."

Abbey laughed, "That's your father telling you all those stories his father once told him".

"Yes but were they all true stories".

Carol laughs, "What about my story? Edwin's coming to whisk me away, a real fairy tale"

"Oh that reminds me your dress"

"Don't worry I have it packed nice and safe".

The door slowly opens and Blake got some fresh water. Everyone gathers around, Blake pours water into various drinking vessels.

"How you feeling Carol the big day has finally arrived?"

"Oh I am so happy, I love Edwin with all my heart".

David heard an unfamiliar sound from outside. "What's that sound, is it the carriage?"

Blake opens the door. "He's here, quickly everyone let us all greet him".

They all walk outside to view an impressive dark carriage now stationary, the large weary white horses taking a well earned rest. The driver places his whip down and then climbs down from the top of the carriage; he then proceeds to open the carriage door. A tall dark hansom educated man climbs out.

"I must humbly apologise as we are so early, you expected us much later did you not?"

"It was quite extraordinary these horses have such pace like a flash of lightning I was here my heart pounding."

Carol opens the door, her features such a comfort to the eye.

"As I was saying my heart pounding, my princess awaiting my arrival".

His eyes were turned full upon her, Carol's eyes glittered and he was intoxicated by her beauty as they walked towards each other and embraced.

Blake and Abbey smiled at each other knowing they had lost their daughter as she was moving to the other side of the country, but the fact they were so in love was a comfort to their hearts. David looked on, his young face glowing with happiness and approval.

Edwin turned his attention to Blake, "I don't want you worrying about your beautiful daughter I will take good care of her".

"Good sir".

Edwin holds out his hand, then Blake reaches out and shakes his warm hand of friendship. Abbey embraces her daughter and David walks over and also embraces his sister as the sorrow starts to sink in. Will he ever see her again? Carol kisses David on the cheek and tears of both sadness and happiness begin to flow.

Edwin takes Carol's hand. "Our carriage awaits us".

The driver collects her belongings and they wave several times, the driver climbs up to his seat the door closes, a crack of a whip and they are on their way. David looks at Abbey as she takes hold of his hand.

"Your going to miss your big sister aren't you David?"

"Yes mum".

Abbey smiles, "Come on Abbey we promised David we would take him to Chester to visit the Midsummer watch, it's such a special day, let us get ready and be on our way.

They all enter their dwelling and dress in their best clothes. Blake collects some shillings out of his old brown box; the sun beats down as they start their journey to Chester. David loves Chester. The Roman walls, the Cathedral city was full of history.

"Come on David catch up and hold my hand".

David starts to run and takes hold of his mum's hand, they are soon entering Chester. In the city the sounds of various musicians echoed all around the streets.

"Look David, Morris dancers!"

David gazes at the colourful performance of the ever popular George and the Dragon. All around happy smiling faces they carried on walking then stopped to watch a parade of giants. David watched in amazement as giant beasts including unicorns, dragons and camels slowly passed by.

Abbey looked to Blake and spoke, "Blake are you going to compete for the golden arrow?".

"No I am out of practice, I am not as good as my father was."

Abbey understood then asked her son, "David do you want to go for a walk around Chester?"

David replied, "Yes."

They then all started to walk along the city streets. The sunlight was bright and warm. David looked up at the black and white buildings and then inhaled the scent of the rose petals. All of a sudden a familiar face appears, its Blake's drinking partner Ralph.

"Hi do you fancy coming to the Blue Bell for a drink?"

Blake looks into Abbeys eyes, his lips were dry, a sudden thirst for ale took control over his mind. After some hesitation Abbey agreed but her heart was filled with bitter disappointment.

"That's that then, me and David better start the long walk home."

They parted and went their separate ways Blake laughs, "Glad you happened to be passing by, you got your cards?"

"Yes, I am going to make me some money".

"You always do Blake, the king of cards, that what they call you. "Good this means I can't loose". Blake pats Ralph on the shoulder and they both start to laugh, then proceed to The Blue Bell Inn. Abbey soon reached home feeling tired she looked to David.

"Lets get inside David, get yourself a drink while I cook us some soup."

David pours water into a cup then drinks until his thirst is quenched. His mother was busy cooking so David walks over to his fathers possessions, he then opens a old box, inside is a pack of old tarot cards. He holds the cards with extraordinary caution, as the cards were delicate and fascinating. David spread out the cards and he gazed at the considerable detail. The star, sun and moon, the hanged man, judgement, temperance. The hermit tower and the devil, he gathered up the pack and pretended to deal the cards to an imaginary friend he would sit quietly and play for hours.

All of a sudden his mother calls his name, "David your soups ready".

David carefully places the pack back into the box and then walks over to the table, where his soup is waiting. He takes a seat, picks up his spoon and starts eating his soup; his mother sits across the table quietly eating her soup. Soon they have both finished and David's eyes start to close.

"It's been a long day, right David off to bed".

David nods his head in agreement and gets into bed; as soon as his small head hits the soft pillow he falls asleep. All of a sudden a loud bang on the door awakens

David it's his father, Blake. Abbey walks over to him and whispers.

"Quiet, David is trying to sleep".

"Look Abbey I've won us lots of money." Blake gets a bag out his pocket and proceeds to empty the contents onto the table. Look over fifty coins. They slowly fall onto the table.

"My god where did you get all those coins from?"

"Oh some drunken noble turned up at the Tavern and challenged me to a game of cards and dice. I took all the money off him, such a born looser."

"Blake, you ought to be careful, he might have kin who disagree with you taking money off him. You know this gambling is illegal, have you no morals?"

"Look Abbey I have amassed a small fortune." Blake walks over to a small wooden box; he opens it and shows Abbey the contents. Her face turned extremely pale as she gazed at the contents of the box, hundreds of coins David watched the horror on his mothers face. "Blake its a small fortune you took all of this money from drunken nobles?"

"Yes".

"Maybe you should stay away from the Blue Bell for a while."

"Maybe your right Abbey, David closed his eyes and embraced the total darkness. Abbey was also tired and made her way to bed.

Blake murmured, "I need my bed also." He glazed at David then got into his bed. The following day, a knock at the door awoke them all; Blake got out of bed and answered the door. It was his friend Ralph.

"Hi Blake have you heard the news?"

"No, what news?"

"That old witch, they found her guilty, she's to be burned at the stake in Broughton."

David hears the conversation, "Dad are you going to watch Hazel the witch burn?"

"No she frightened you didn't she?"

"Yes she talked about voices, I believe she was in league with the devil".

"Abbey are you all right, you're not saying much?"

"Oh I am not feeling too good, I feel sick."

"Abbey go on lie down and get some rest," David get dressed and we shall go for a walk so your mother can get some sleep".

Abbey got back into her bed, Ralph stood by the door awaiting his friend.

"Blake lets take a walk to the market and get some fresh vegetables". David is dressed ready to go to the market whilst Abbey peacefully sleeps. They soon return home and Blake calls out his wives name.

"Abbey! I have returned with fresh vegetables, are you better now?" The room remained silent.

"Abbey wake up!"

Blake lifted up the cover that was pulled over her head, he shrieked in horror then became hysterical.

"My god stay back, your mothers dead, a victim of the plague!"

David looked into his father's eyes as they began to glisten with tears.

"Come on son, we need to inform Father Ryan, it's the Black Death, your mothers dead."

David gazed at him open mouthed in total disbelief it was all like a bad dream. David and his father left Abbey and went to seek out Father Ryan, The Father and a group of men removed the dead body they then set fire to the corpse. Blake couldn't get over the death of Abbey and sort out the comfort of drink.

"David stay here, I am meeting Ralph at the Blue Bell for a game of cards". David looked up at his father frightened he was about to loose him as well as his mother.

"Look son I wont be long, Ralph wants to see me I promise tomorrow we will leave here and visit your sister Carol in Dover."

David watched as his father left, a sense of doom engulfed his every move. Blake met up with Ralph in Chester in the usual watering hole the Blue Bell. Blake entered the Blue Bell seeking out his friend. Ralph was already waiting, cards and dice at the ready.

The noise of drunken intoxication echoed all around, Blake noticed a tall dark stranger sitting next to Ralph. Blake walked towards them his heart pounding, something wasn't right he stared at the stranger worriedly.

"Hi Ralph who is this then?"

The stranger spoke quietly. Sit down and listen to what I am about to tell you, my name is Myles Mason, my brother Jacob has told me all about you, god rest his soul He was a fool a drunk, he gambled his money away in a drunken state so I am led to believe when he lost in cards he became even more drunk, now he is dead."

"How did he die?"

"Oh such a terrible accident he fell off his horse drunk landing on his head, his neck snapped like a twig. If he hadn't lost all his money I believe he would still be alive today."

All of a sudden two large men moved closer from the shadows. "Justice is a solemn friend of mine who abides by the rules, you sir do not". His face changed to anger. "I have paid these two assassins. My brother is no longer of this world, my friend you will soon be joining him."

Blake looked at the assassins, both complete with weapons the one on the left, a face full of scars, dark piercing eyes, his fellow assassin of large build, discoloured skin and eyes of pure evil.

Blake looked to his friend Ralph his heart was pounding; deep down he knew it was the end. Blake slowly rose to his feet, the stranger spoke. "You look so horror stricken, and so you should be, these assassins have never failed at their chosen profession but unlike you I am a generous man, I will give you a head start leave this place and run for your life."

Blake felt shaken and dazed, a panic of abject terror filled his mind and soul. Blake moved swiftly out of the

Bluebell Inn and then towards Watergate Street, somehow one of the assassins had managed to cut off his flight path. Blake watched frozen, motionless as the assassin moved in for the kill with his sword raised high. Blake turned around ready to evade the assassin. To his complete horror the second assassin stood silently behind him Blake looked into his cold barbaric eyes, in a split second a savage blow. Blake's eyelids flickered spasmodically, blood poured from a wound to his neck; he fell backwards onto the cold surface nearly decapitated. His eyes closed and his heart beat no more. David sat awaiting his fathers return, anxiety twisted his face as he knew something wasn't right.

All of a sudden a knock on the door, David opens it there before him stood a familiar face, it was Father Ryan. David gazed at him worried, his poor heart was pounding. Come here David you need to come with me something has happened to your father.

David began to shake and weep hysterically.

"He's dead isn't he?"

"Yes David he's dead his gambling finally caught up with him."

"Was it the noble my father won money off?"

"No he is also dead."

"What about my fathers friend Ralph, he must know something?"

"I am afraid Ralph has disappeared without trace. The nobles brother, your father took money from, I have been informed he was present at the Blue Bell Inn but he is a good man honest, always donating money to the Church. I will send word to your older sister in Dover"

"Me and my father were to travel there tomorrow".

"Your father's money. Ill-gotten gains, where did he keep his silver coins? The Church will take the money, it will help rest your fathers soul."

David showed Father Ryan the box of coins, the priest opened the box; he smiled to himself in contentment.

"This is a tidy sum young David, let us leave, you can stay with me until your sister collects you. Be brave for your departed parents sake," he spoke in a low calming voice. The two of them left moving swiftly without noise David wiped the tears from his eyes as the priest escorted him to his humble dwelling. "This way David".

They entered the old cottage.

"Here David this will be your room. Oh such is the sadness that has engulfed your world," Father Ryan placed the precious box of coins on top of his dark oak table he then reached for a book. He then turned to David.

"Here, this book will guide you through your life on earth it's the Bible. I want you to read it when you are older and wiser here my gift to you". Father Ryan handed the book to David he took tight hold and in a low voice he expressed his gratitude.

"The Lord be praised; now we both need some sleep". Father Ryan opened the door to a bedroom, go in David climb into bed and sleep I will awake you in the morning. David clutched tight hold of the Bible he walked over to the bed and then climbed into it pulling the cover over his head David fell into a deep sleep. He dreamt of his departed parents, they spoke to him telling him they had entered a better place free from evil and decay. An angel appeared her whole body glowing a flooding of light above her head she spoke of having faith in the five fives the five avars. Health, vital, karmic, character, and spiritual.

"Listen to what I say, you are only young do I talk beyond your comprehension? Your sister will come for you tomorrow I have told her to look after you; education is your path forward. I must go now never tell anyone that I visit you in your sleep they wouldn't understand".

The angel slowly disappeared from David's dream waving as she disappeared. David's eyes opened and he looked to a small window where the sun shone in all its radiant glory. Father Ryan appeared opening the bedroom door slowly.

"Hi David did you have a nice sleep, your sister Carol shall be arriving later".

David's mind began to fill with excitement he nodded in confirmation, David longed to see his older sister again he was missing his mother and father.

"Come this way David and I will fix you up with some bread and water".

David got out of the bed and followed Father Ryan to the dinning area, the area was dark. David looked up at the dark oak beams and on the walls, pictures of saints.

"David this way," Father Ryan proceeded to pull out a chair, David sat down whilst Father Ryan passed him a drink of water.

"Right David you wait here whilst I cut you up some bread".

Father Ryan walked out of the room to the kitchen to collect the bread as David gazed around the room at the various pictures one in particular caught his eye. The Virgin Mary in all her radiant glory was she the angel David saw in his dreams.

All of a sudden father Ryan appeared with the pre-cut bread. "Here you are David look what I found; you left it on your bed."

"Oh my Bible".

"Remember always keep it by you".

David held out his hand and the father placed it in his hand.

"Right I will say a short prayer and you can tuck into your bread". Father Ryan says a short prayer and then says amen. David slowly picks up some bread and begins to eat it; the bread was fresh and delicious. All of a sudden, a knock on the door.

"Oh David hopefully that will be your sister Carol."

Father Ryan answered the door to his relief it was indeed Carol.

"Hi you have travelled a long way please come inside and have a drink? David will be so glad to see you after the sad departure of his mother and father."

Carol drew a deep breath. "They were my mother and father as well, my mother I know died of the plague but my father murdered by assassins in Watergate Street."

"Who said anything about assassins he had been gambling I believe he was robbed".

"What was the cause of death?"

"The poor man, god rest his soul, was almost decapitated it must have been a sword."

"Strange there's not many thieves armed with swords."

"Yes I must admit it is a mystery".

"What of his collection of silver coins?"

"Oh after his poor wife died he confessed to me about his gambling and asked me if anything should happen to him, he wanted me to have the silver as a donation to the Church. His soul was troubled riddled with guilt; gambling is such a sin in the eyes of God".

Carol gazed into his eyes knowing he had lied about the silver. Her father would never have donated his precious silver to the Church but there was nothing she could do about it, the word of the Church was all too powerful. "Where is David he hasn't been donated to the Church?"

"No, his destiny is to be with you in his new home in Dover hopefully he is to be educated in the ways of our good Lord; this way Carol."

They both proceed to the dinning room where David had just consumed the rest of his bread. Father Ryan opened the door, "Look David a friendly face it's your sister!"

David looked up and saw her warm smiling face, he jumped to his feet a feeling of wild amazement, his eyes began to glisten with tears. His heart was pounding he embraced his sister she kissed his cheek.

"Oh how I am glad to see you, you're coming to Dover with me. Outside is a carriage awaiting. Look David don't cry I know all about our mother and father but we must put all this behind us. I am here to give you a fresh start I am going to get you a real education".

Father Ryan hands Carol some refreshing water. "Thank you father she drinks the water then hands the empty drinking vessel to the father."

"So you will be on your way now, have a pleasant journey remember your Bible David."

"Yes I have it here in my hand."

"Good bye, bye Carol and David it's a better place you leave for."

Carol takes David by the hand and they proceed to the waiting carriage. A tall coachman dressed all in black opens the door Carol ushers David into the coach. The golden sunlight gleamed in the early afternoon, they sat embracing each other a loud crack of the whip, the noise pounded in David's ears with great haste they were on long path to Dover. Carol told David about how she had boarded a ship from Dover to France. She was now married to Edwin Smith and they lived in a farmhouse complete with acres of orchards and gardens she told David about the chickens, ducks and geese they had kept. For her husband was a wealthy man.

"Will Edwin mind me coming to live with you?"

"No I have explained to him about our father and mothers demise.

I promised our mother if anything happened to them then I would look after you until you were able to fend for yourself".

It was a long journey to Dover David gazed out of the carriage to the wind swept trees; all of a sudden Carol spoke. "David are you alright? Sometimes you look so distant we are nearly at your new home. Look David at those golden fields of Barley."

All of a sudden, the sun appeared again in all of its glory David smiles he remembered the angel had told him it was his destiny to be in Dover and education was the key. The carriage came to a halt. David's eyes peeked with curiosity as Carol offered David her hand.

"Come with me my little brother".

The door opened and they both proceeded to climb out the tall dark figure stood motionless near to a doorway. It was Edwin he slowly moved towards them then spoke with a calm voice. "Good morning young sir I hope your journey was a pleasant one".

David now knew Edwin had good heart Carol smiled and rushed over to her husband to embrace him David looked on with approval Edwin then spoke.

"My mother has cooked all of us a great feast you both must be ravenous with hunger. Come in I have drinks to quench your thirsts."

They all walked into the large dwelling inside the dinning room was Edwin's mother. She was old but her radiant smile left David completely unnerved. He smiled to himself in contentment she then spoke.

"Young David I have heard so much about you, young sir this is your seat."

A large oak table with matching chairs, the floorboards creaked as David walked the short distance to his seat. He sat down and they all greeted each other then the drink and food arrived.

"Here you are David, roast beef and vegetables".

David had never seen such food and started to fill his empty stomach. They all then sat around after the meal making a decision about David's education. After some debate it was decided David would be sent to Oxford to be educated.

Carol looked at David. "I promised our departed parents I would have you properly educated, Oxford is where you will achieve much greatness. It is late I will show you to your room come David take my hand".

Everyone smiled then David climbed from his chair and proceeded to thank everyone for their kindness. David took hold of his sister's hand and they both left the room with echoes of goodnight following David's every step. They walked down a corridor the floorboards continued to creek. David looked up at the solid oak beams then his eyes became permanently fixed on an old dark wooden door Carol opened the door.

"Look David this is to be your room until I visit Oxford to arrange your education".

David knew his sister had his best interests at heart. The room was dark, the bed was large.

"David this is our guest room, look over there on the table I have brought you some new clothes to wear".

David remembered his Bible, had he left it in the carriage.

"David you look confused, as if you have lost something, maybe a book?"

David smiled.

"Look towards the pillow on your bed".

To David's amazement there was his lost Bible.

"The coachman gave it to me".

Carol picked up the Bible; it was written in Latin, she flicked through the pages until she came to a prayer, which she proceeded to read out. David stood motionless and gazed up at his sister, in his eyes she was but an angel. Carol smiled then handed the book to David.

"Soon I will have you reading Latin and then this book will have true meaning to you".

David placed the Bible under his pillow then climbed into his bed his sister kissed him on the cheek.

"Goodnight David, it has been such a long day".

David closed his eyelids and was soon fast asleep. David was soon visiting the land of dreams where he could see both his mother and father, they waved to him hand in hand and they walked along a golden landscape finally sharing everlasting peace together.

All of a sudden the bedroom door opened and Carol walked in, she opened the window and the morning sun shone through in all of its glory.

"Morning sleepy head".

David opened his eyes then climbed out of bed onto the cold floor.

"Did you have a nice sleep?"

"Yes I dreamt of our parents. I saw them walking holding hands together forever in Heaven".

"David do you often dream?"

"Yes I dream of angels".

"Do angels sometimes visit you in your sleep?"

"Good they visit me as well. I know lets quickly try on your new clothes I am taking you to Oxford. I have many friends at the college, you will be welcomed with open arms the sooner you start, the better."

David walked over to his new clothes, he had never felt such fine materials and all of the clothes fitted him to perfection; his sister had done him proud.

"Oh David what a transformation you now look like a gentleman."

"Thank you Carol the clothes are truly amazing".

"Right have we forgotten anything? We just need to find you some boots".

Carol opened an old oak chest and inside were a pair of boots. "I think they are your size". She handed the boots to David, who proceeded to try them on.

"Are they all right?"

"Well there a little on the large side".

"Oh well you should grow into them. I have prepared us a breakfast this way David."

He picked up his Bible and then followed his sister to the dinning area where they had breakfast and then walked the short distance to where the coach was waiting to take them to Oxford, a crack of a whip and they were soon on their way. David's heart was pounding he drew a deep breath.

"Are you all right David?"

She spoke with a voice filled with concern. "Everybody becomes nervous, I was the same but I have picked out a good catholic college. Edwin's friend has assured us that you will be educated to the highest standards and when you return from college you will be reading and writing ready to fulfil your destiny."

David trusted his sister as she spoke with such confidence and honestly. Several days later they arrive at the college in Oxford and David knew deep down he would adapt to his new surroundings.

Carol spoke with a low voice. "Are you feeling better now?"

"Yes I won't let you down, I will study hard and try my best".

David said good bye to his sister and then began his education. He studied Greek religion and mathematics; very soon he was speaking Latin and writing in ink, copying the alphabet and the Lords Prayer.

David would often be found in the library as he had a real thirst for knowledge. Science, magic and astrology, the teachers were very strict and misbehaving pupils were often beaten with the birch. Although David kept himself to himself and the teachers were so impressed with his progress they contacted Carol who visited him to his total delight. The years flew by quickly.

David was reaching twenty-five years of age and he knew it was time to return to Dover. He finished his education top in every subject he had studied. A coach brought him back to Dover and he arrived to find Edwin and Carol standing in the doorway waiting to greet him, in his hand, the Bible he was given by Father Ryan. He was greeted by two warm smiling faces as he climbed out of the carriage and walked towards them.

Carol spoke, "You kept your promise, you've returned a tall handsome well educated man".

David smiled and spoke with confidence, "Look I still have the Bible written in Latin, the difference is that I can now read it!"

"Good come inside we must talk of your future".

David followed them inside they all sat around the oak table Carol looked over to David and spoke, "Tomorrow is your twenty-fifth birthday!"

David laughs. "I am really that old!"

"Yes and Edwin would like to know now that you have a top-class education if you would like to come and work for him? If not he could find you a job with one of his associates"

Utter silence filled the room, David was lost for words. "I am sorry I am in total shock I was not expecting offers of work, my heart is set on a visit to France."

"That's all right David. I've been to France. Paris the capital is such a beautiful city; if your heart is set on France then we will discuss work when you return. Here David some wine."

Carol stands up and pours wine into three drinking vessels she then passes a drink to David and Edwin. Everyone makes a toast to David's education. They take a sip of wine reminiscing about the past, soon darkness fills the room Carol lights some candles on the table and David starts to yawn.

"Oh someone is very tired, you know where the guest room is don't you?"

"Yes I remember; its time for my bed."

They all wish each other a good nights sleep David stands up and the effects of the wine make him a little light headed he walks off in the direction of the guest room along the dark corridor. He lights the candle and then opens the door and heads straight for the bed then collapses onto it. After blowing the candle out the room turns to total darkness. He soon entered his realm of dreams and then ventured to the fifth dimension in this dream.

He met up with a tall strange looking man, all of a sudden he spoke, "My name is Cavoc, I have much to tell you the year is fifteen twenty-five in five hundred years to this day the world will end. I hear you are now educated, although the details on how the world will end are very complex, as you already know France is the key. Seek out a friend of mine, his name is Nostradamme will show you the key to your destiny. I want you to visit me in the fifth dimension, this wise man will be your guide to my dimension".

His voice was dominating; David drew a deep breath and the apparition disappeared. He opened his eyes to see a picture of an angel, which hung on the wall opposite the window gleaming in the early sunlight. David gazed at the emulation of the picture; France was his destiny He threw off his covers and jumped out of bed getting dressed whilst the word Nostradamme rang out in his ears.

He was soon dressed and he opened the door and looked towards the end of the corridor, there walking towards him was his sister Carol. He knew it was time to leave for France. Drawing a deep breath he approached her.

"David you are leaving, are you leaving now?"

"Yes France is my destiny."

"I know, I have prearranged everything the coach arrives in one hour there you will board a boat across the English Channel for France.

"How did you know?"

"A man visited me in the realms of my dreams he told me to assist you to fulfil your destiny."

David thanked his sister, they embraced and then she kissed him on the cheek. With his usual composure he enquired, "What is for breakfast?"

"This way David I will cook you some eggs".

David walked over to the dinning area and sat down at the table, his sister proceeded to the kitchen and David poured out a drink of water and awaited his sister. Breakfast was ready in no time; Carol placed the hot meal on the table next to David. He soon ate the food placed in front of him.

"Thank you sister that was truly delicious."

Carol then reached out for a bag of coins

"Here David you will need money for your travels around France."

"Oh what can I say yet again you have truly spoilt me," tears trickled down her cheeks.

"Wipe away those tears I want to leave with a vision of your happy smiling face, no tears." Carol started to laugh out loud and they both embraced once more. There was then a knock at the door it was the coachman. Carol then embraced her brother for the last time. "Remember happy smiling face! Wait your Bible?"

"I've left it in the bedroom keep it there until the day I return.

Carol smiles and laughs as she watches David climb onto the carriage. They waved as the carriage was soon on its way. The sunlight was warm and bright and David's face was glowing with anticipation. All of a sudden the carriage came to a halt the door opens and a tall dark figure appears.

"Sir we have reached the Port your boat to France awaits you".

"Thank you driver".

David climbed out of the carriage and then gazed at the boat he then scanned all around, anxiety clouded his face, he had never ventured out on a boat before. The saving grace was that the sea was calm. A snub-nosed man with a long face shouted over. "This way Sir I am to take you to France".

David waded out into the sea and climbed aboard the boat. The sea was cold, inside the boat a disagreeable damp smell. David turned extremely pale as he caught his breath and then sat back.

"You all right Sir?"

"Yes".

"First time in a boat is it Sir?"

"Yes."

Another rower a young fresh-faced silent stocky man started to row. Seagulls glided in the sky above the boat their piercing cries and the crash of the waves upon the side of the boat left David in a trace-like state, he sat rooted with fear. A peculiar shiver crossed him, his mouth was dry, tiredness set in and his eyes began to close.

Later he opened them to find out his ordeal was nearly over.

"Dry land sir, we are nearly there you've been asleep for ages, must be the salty air".

"I can't wait to set foot on dry land".

The rowers put their backs into the rowing and soon David arrived on French soil. On the beach stood a tall dark figure his hand beckoning David. He climbed out of the boat then waded determinedly towards the mysterious dark figure.

A voice in the background spoke, "Goodbye master I'll let your sister know you set foot on the French soil safely."

The mysterious stranger walked towards David then spoke in a deep cold gravely voice. "My name is Mabus I am here at your service. Master Cavoc has instructed me to be your guide".

David looked upon his weather-beaten malignant face in a confused state.

"You say Cavoc is your master?"

"Yes he comes to me in my dreams as he does with you, so he isn't but a dream believe me he is real, you are special to him, he wants you to pass over to his dimension. He has something he must share with you, riches beyond your wildest dreams you are interested are you not?"

"Yes he told me I had to find a man by the name of Nostradame do you know where I could find such a man?"

"Yes Nostradame as he is known, is famed as a mathematician astrologer and physician. At present he is a Montpellier studying medicine since the death of his wife and children. He has become a bit of a wonderer and we will find him in Montpellier".

David drew another deep breath and then spoke.

"I must admit without you my mission would be of a lost cause".

"Good then everything is settled; this way I have a carriage awaiting at the top of the cliff, this way".

David followed Mabus as he circumnavigated the rough dry grass and nettles whilst climbing to the top of the cliff. Once at the top Mabus pointed to the awaiting carriage complete with a driver.

"This way David".

They arrive at the carriage Mabus opens the door and they both climb in and sit down.

"David you must keep your wits about you at all times, France is corrupt. Devil worship amongst the rich is rife".

All of a sudden the carriage starts to move on its joinery to Montpelier.

"David, Nostradame is special, he has visited the master in the fifth dimension he will show you the way. The number five is special as well, all of us have five senses hearing, sight, taste, touch and smell. The law of the fives states that simply all things happen in fives, or are divisible by or are multiples of five or are somehow directly or indirectly appropriate to five. In Greek orthodox Christian mysticism the number five symbolises the Holy Spirit as the bearer of all life. The book of psalms is arranged into five books paralleling the five books of Moses. Muslims pray to Allah five times a day. Five is conjectured to be the only odd untouchable number and if this is the case the five will be the only odd prime number that is not the aliquot of a three. I was born in fifteen hundred my age is twenty-five, Cavoc visited me in my dreams and my he told me the world would end in five hundred years. The year two thousand and twenty-five".

All of this is correct Cavoc believes these are dark ages where great thinkers are to be persecuted in the fifth dimension, he knows of the balance between good and evil. Religion is the greatest evil; the church is at war with everyone that studies philosophy, science and spiritualism, the sentence is torture then a horrible death. Just remember there are eyes and ears everywhere now. Have you got any questions?"

"Yes is Cavoc a God in his dimension?"

"Yes he is immortal, and powerful. One thing you must remember he is good and evil, a balance of the two. Now it is getting dark we must try to get some sleep".

The journey was long and David woke up to the sound of the carriage travelling at great speed and the gale force wind howling all around.

A draught of cold air, a sudden chill ran down his spine and the carriage was subject to violent vibrations. All of a sudden Mabus opens his eyes.

"Good morning did you sleep well?"

"Yes".

The carriage came to a sudden halt.

"That will be the thieves I guarantee if you travel along these roads you will meet up with thieves at least once. Cavoc has told me that I must protect you with my life; you must stay in the carriage whilst I have a quiet word with them. Do not fear I have killed many thieves in my lifetime. Move over to that seat, I have my weapon underneath it".

David moved whilst Mabus bent down and pulled out a long box, he then opened it. Inside was a long sword.

"Nice is it not? The weapon once belonged to a Knight Templar, it has shed much blood".

David gazed at the engraving on the sword it was pure perfection.

"Remember no matter what happens you must stay in the carriage".

David gazed into his cold eyes and fear engulfed his every thought, the carriage door creaked as Mabus opened the door, he then closed the door slowly. He could hear Mabus, his voice dominating, David's curiosity got the better of him he slowly opened the carriage door to witness two men on horses one dismounted, he had a crossbow pointed at Mabus the other two were armed with swords Mabus spoke again.

"Get back on your horses and leave us; be gone and no harm will come to you".

The man with the crossbow's face became twisted with anxiety and he shook with impatience all of a sudden his anger erupted like a volcano.

"Give me your money or you die now".

Mabus laughs out loud, "My master would not allow such madness".

The carriage driver sat motionless frozen with fear. David looked on at the thieves' barbaric complexions; in a split second the thief fired the bolt from his crossbow. Mabus jumped into the air evading the bolt and he moved swiftly towards the thief who looked on in disbelief. Mabus swung his sword with animal like strength two savage blows and the thief fell to the ground, blood pouring from his wounds, his wailing choking screams echoed all around.

His friends looked on filled with fear, Mabus screamed at the top of his voice. "Leave or share the same fate as this sorry fool."

The thieves on the horses looked at each other then to their fallen Comrade their eyes full of fear at what they had just witnessed. All of a sudden panic set in and they galloped back into the forest with great haste. Mabus turned around and looked at David, he then spoke with his usual dominating voice. "You must obey my instructions I told you to stay in the carriage for your own safety do as I say".

"Cavoc would punish me if anything were to happen to you".

"I am sorry David looked at the crusader sword, it has yet again spilled blood in a just cause."

"Mabus is he dead?"

Completely"

The savage blows had left the thief's mutilated body motionless; a strange silence enveloped the scene of death.

"Mabus what about the body?"

"Justice has been dealt, let the animals of the forest feed on his rotting corpse."

David looked into his cold dark eyes.

"Let us be on our way".

David climbed on to the carriage as Mabus signalled to the driver to carry on with the journey then entered the carriage and closed the door behind him, he wiped the blood off the sword and he placed it back in the wooden box, he then turned to David and spoke. "Look David, life is but a harsh reality, I know both of your parents died cruel deaths your mother, the black death and then your father slain on the streets of Chester by assassins".

"You know so much about me yet I know so little about you">

A brief silence, Mabus smiled to himself in contentment uninterrupted Mabus spoke. "Anger and sorrow fill my cold heart, Cavoc spoke to me in my dream as he did with you, I too have lost special ones".

"My wife and son died of the plague my master was slain by Jew's. I was ready to end it all when

Cavoc instructed me in the faith of the five fives, you are the chosen prophet one of your bloodline will spread the gospel of the new age that is about to dawn."

David gazed into his black cold eyes, his face extremely pale he felt his mouth go dry.

"David you look confused there is a lot to take in but Cavoc will go into greater detail, in several days we will arrive at Montpellier we shall eat and drink then locate Nostradame. I have read books on the dark arts and believe the devil walks amongst us. In this century evil is all about us. Suddenly, the darkness outside was almost total, the light from the full moon captivated David's eye and then a shriek so, horrid the piecing cry of the wolf. David became frightened. He looked out of the carriage window his mind paralysed by the hideous sight, his fingers began to twitch and then a low voice completely unnerved him.

"Do not concern yourself they will not harm us."

"Are they wolves? I once read about these beasts there have been thousands of reported cases all over Europe."

"Yes I read too, as I have said these are evil times".

The carriage began to speed up as the driver became gripped with panic. The crack of the whip Mabus begins to laugh. "The wolves have had the desired effect on the driver we shall arrive even sooner. David soon regained his composure as they entered the cobbled streets of

Montpellier; the cries of the wolves soon became a distant memory.

"David we are now in Montpellier how are you?"

"I am feeling exhausted hungry and thirsty."

"That makes two of us, our needs will be seen to very shortly."

All of a sudden the carriage ground to a halt. Mabus opened the door of the carriage; it was daylight once more they both stepped out on to the cobble road. David looked around at the medieval stone buildings.

"David look over there at the cathedral of St Pierre, it was built in thirteen forty-six, the twin church towers are amazing it is one of the greatest architecture masterpieces.

"You alright my friend it is truly magnificent".

The driver without a word disappeared into the shadows and then from the alleyway a familiar face a friend of Mabus.

"Oh David this is James he will take us to his house."

James approached wide-eyed complete with a gleaming smile. "Pleasant journey my friend?"

"Yes".

"And let me guess this young man must be David?"

He extends his hand in friendship and they shake hands. "This way".

The streets were narrow full and of people going about their business, David looked up at the Gothic style building with carvings of saints.

"This way through this door."

They all walk through a heavy oak engraved door, inside the room dark solid oak beams, pictures hanging on all four walls, the furniture was well worn.

"What's that smell?"

"Oh I make it myself Mutton Broth."

"It smells divine".

"Good".

James was an easy-going person complete with a long thin face and odd sized clothes.

"All right my friends please take a seat and I will get you some broth".

David and Mabus sat down awaiting their food, very soon James appeared with the assistance of a young lady. Mabus laughs, "Are you sure your the cook James?"

"Well this is my niece Diana she loves cooking so I said she could lend me a hand!"

David looks over at Diana, a small petite shy faced girl.

"Oh Diana, words are something she lacks when strangers are present. David laughs as she hurries back to the kitchen. James also sits and they all start to eat. Diana returns with an opened bottle of wine and three goblets on a tray, she places them on the table and with a blink of an eye she disappears again. James pours wine for his friends then sits back.

"Mabus, great news, I have contacted Nostradame he is staying at the old merchant's house and he awaits David with great anticipation."

"David how do you feel, will you see him today or tomorrow?"

"Destiny waits for no man. Your mutton broth and good wine have given me a new lease of life; show me the way to Nostradame. I have heard so much about him."

"He is captivated by philosophical theories of the day and has superior intelligence, Nostradame is in Montpellier studying for his bachelors degree in medicine. I will take you to see him".

"What about you Mabus?"

"I will await your return and drink a little more wine."

They all laugh and then James opens the door closely followed by David. They then walk for a short while; there were pilgrims everywhere passing through Montpellier to the North. David moved in and out of the crowds until James movements ground to a halt.

"This is the merchants' house. Nostradame is inside waiting". David looked towards the window; there was a tall dark figure that moved with great haste towards the door, it opened slightly.

"I will await your return, do not fear Nostradame, he is a good man."

David entered with great fascination and he felt a cool breeze on the back of his neck as he closed the door behind him. There before him stood a pale bearded man dressed all in black.

"You must be the one Cavoc told me about, you must be David. I have awaited your arrival, as you well know I am Nostradame this way follow me".

David walked upon a scarlet carpet; the room was decorated with strange tapestries and pictures. Nostradame opened the door inside a special spiral staircase.

"This way David to my secret chamber".

David followed Nostradame up the stairs not knowing what to expect. They both soon reached the top. David looked all around he saw giant bookshelves filled with all kinds of books from bygone ages; magic, medicine, occult and astrology.

"David I see you have an eye for my books, one day you may have such a fine collection".

David then turned his attention to a three-legged brass stool on the far side of the room.

"Ah you have noticed the brass stool, a key instrument in your journey to the fifth dimension, this way my friend"

David looked at Nostradame in confusion, although he followed with great anticipation.

"David take a seat and take off your boots".

David sat down and removed his boots.

"Right David I have filled this bowl with water".

Nostradame picked up a bowl of water from behind an old table and placed it beneath David's feet.

"The water may be a little cold".

David placed his feet into the water; a sudden chill ran up his spine taking his breath away.

"Right now David on the table I have prepared a drink I am amongst other things an alchemist, I have mixed various herbs and potions, the end result is a drink that will expand your brain function. You look lost, logic is so demanding is it not".

Nostradame hands the drink to David he hesitates then takes a drink, a strange sensation, a feeling of enlightenment.

"Congratulations I owe you my gratitude we are nearly complete".

Nostradame picked up his Laurel then proceeded to recite an ancient spell. All of a sudden, David's hand and feet began to shake vigorously, his face frozen with fear, a series of macabre visions, he shivered throughout his frame blinking and frowning, then a flash of blinding bright lights. His eyes are completely closed, then in a total calm quiet and stillness he begins to open his eyes, a sensation of warmth, a feeling of wild amazement now with eyes wide open. He looked to his feet beneath them clear, warm, golden soft sand he then looked above; a quick glimpse of the sky, the stars shinning brightly, the moon was large and it gave off a bright glare of light. He looked all around with fixed fascination, he stepped abruptly and caught his breath, all around him a strange landscape, he could see mountains of white in the distance.

All of a sudden, David noticed a mysterious figure, his hand stretched out beckoning David forward, the atmosphere was strange, he moved at a slow pace, a sense of enlightenment engulfed his every move; closer and closer he moved towards the tall figure. David was now close, he looked at the figure steadily in the face, a tall man with a pale complexion and eyes of green, he sat upon a golden throne dressed in white. On his head sat a shiny golden crown complete with priceless gems, suddenly the tall man stood up and spoke with a dominant deep voice. "My name is Cavoc you gaze upon me, yes I am as pale as the moon, tall with large piercing eyes of emerald green. On my forehead a scar; it was my third eye, you shall see it at a latter date the eye of Cavoc. I am the creator immortal and of superior intelligence, we have much to get through take a seat David."

"What seat?"

"Behind you David".

David turns confused, there before him lay a golden throne encrusted with precious jewels.

"Nice is it not? This once belonged to Cleopatra, Queen of Egypt. Such beauty was her downfall as was love affairs with Roman War Lords Julius Caesar and Mark Anthony. She died after drinking a mixture of hemlock, wolfs-bane and opium."

"How do you know so much Cavoc?"

"Because I was there of course, I have walked across your domain since the dawn of time, go on its quite safe to sit on".

David sat on the golden throne.

"It feels good doesn't it?"

David regained his composure; his mind was full of curiosity.

"Are you sitting comfortably?"

"Yes".

"Good I will continue with my story, I met up with Moses his people and his brother Aaron, Moses unleashed plagues then escaped Egypt separating the red sea, such an amazing spectacle, they all passed through dry land to safely. Later I met up with Moses again, he was writing the first five books of the Bible, we watched as a bush was engulfed by flames and we talked together on Mount Horeb and Sinai we had our disagreements on the stories he was writing, the rest is history. The book will be so popular in the twentieth century, there will be billions of copies perhaps Moses was right. Later on another book came to my attention I have the original here, again a book of true power a Jew wrote it. Inside this book is the ultimate formula, the transformation of lead to gold, the metal of the gods, the Jews used this book to mass produce gold they paid their taxes to the Roman emperors the gold kept them in good favour. The Jews lived across the Roman empire in relative harmony.

"I came along and stole the book before Dogon the demon could get hold of it, he was so angry the emperors without gold became hostile and then began the persecution of the Jews. Cabal was tortured and crucified and then six priests where put to death. A dozen wealthy priests united, he often slept with Jewish whores, one in particular by the name of Delia was paid to poison Dogon. She placed enough poison in his wine to kill ten men. It left him in a state of unconsciousness, five assassins with sacred silver daggers then entered his dwelling lead by Jacob, they stabbed him more than fifty times, they then left his mutated body with great haste.

"High priest Na-dab had a vision of Dogon's spirit reborn inflicting revenge on the Jewish people, he sent all of his men back and he informed them that they must cremate the body to prevent his evil being reborn. They were met by a small Roman army, the body was gone, a high priestess of the dark arts Hegel and her followers moved the body to Europe the Jewish masses rioted and wiped out a small Roman garrison six hundred and sixty-six Romans died; revenge was swift. The fifth legion was deployed to crush the revolt Delia and Na-dab and the five were taken alive tortured and then beheaded. The Romans carried on killing Jews until one million lay dead.

"David I know what you are thinking it was all down to me for I was the one who stole the book. But imagine if Dogon had got his hands on it, he had plans to build up the greatest war chest of the age, gold would have given him the power to control and dominate the world," Cavoc smiled.

"Right I shall continue, I met Jesus when he was feeding the five thousand with five loafs of bread. A priest informed me of his relationship with Mary

Magdalene. Jesus described her as his concubine; she sat on the right of Jesus during the Last Supper. I instructed Leonardo de Vinci on his painting; after all I knew the seating arrangements as I was at the Last Supper. Everyone is frightened of religious persecution, it's the evil in mankind. I informed Jesus he was about to be betrayed by Judas but he just wouldn't listen.

"Judas, Jesus, Romans then death on a cross, during the crucifixion Jesus suffered from five wounds. Mary Magalene travelled to Gaul. I was very fond of her, she was wealthy, honourable respectable and loyal. She travelled with friends I believe she was bearing a child; the ultimate bloodline was Joan of Arc of the same bloodline maybe, maybe not; the thing I craved the most was the Grail.

"What a treasure I remember searching for it feverishly it had simply disappeared. Centuries later, the crusaders, Christian armies who put to death large numbers of Muslims and Jews in the name of Religion.

"Brothers William and Henry and their Knights Templar located the grail and were on the way to Europe with the precious cargo. I was so angry, I wanted it so badly so I met up with them killing a dozen knights before it was mine. Look I have it here beside me. David gazed at the sinister expression on Cavoc's face, cautiously David moved off his seat, "No need to get up here, catch!"

Cavoc tossed the Holy Grail to David, he managed to catch it, the relief on his face was so clear.

"Examine it, I am afraid only dry traces of blood remain I should have found it earlier is it not impressive?"

David couldn't believe it he was holding the ultimate treasure the Holy Grail.

"When you have finished looking at it, gently place it on the floor beside you, I remember the fifth century, it was a time of turmoil the druids and the pagans died a death along with the Roman Empire. This is the fifth dimension, it is governed by good and evil; everything that dwells in your imagination your worst nightmares. For example the beast, the devil and also the good; a saint, or an angel and so on. I have passed over to your domain at will.

"I have many talents, one is shape-shifting. I can blend in wherever it is necessary in any given situation. For many full moons I have entered your domain with my pets they reap havoc feast and return".

A look of pure horror is on David's face.

"You are in a state of shock, we all reap the seeds of good and evil".

David summons up the courage to speak his mind.

"Cavoc millions live in fear and thousands have died, your beasts have truly reaped havoc all over Europe."

"Do not concern yourself, soon all of this will come to pass, your world has evolved, your weapons are becoming more and more advanced, your people more organised in the fight against evil.

"In the centuries to come the passage to your domain will become impossible. Cavoc there is evil in your eyes why should I help you?"

"The evil in my eyes; once upon a time there was no evil in my eyes, the curse of mankind has taken its toll on me. I have witnessed such evil and decay in your domain".

Anger and sorrow filled his cold heart, "Like my realm I am a mixture of good and evil if you help me I promise eventually good will conquer over evil".

"How is my dearest friend Nostradamus he is such a great man without him you would not be sitting before me now."

"Cavoc I believe his name is Nostradame".

"Not for long, I have the power to predict future events Nostradamus' reward for helping me will be a book, he will complete in fifteen hundred and fifty-five predicting the future, I will help him become the greatest seer of all time. He will be worshipped by millions in the centuries ahead. Let us go back to the book cabal the Jew wrote. I want you to have it and keep it close to you, protect it with you life. As we speak your trusted friends Mabus and James have enlisted the help of Duval Wolfe a very important alchemist. I am convinced he will translate the words and pictures in this precious book. Also Lucas Lopez an expert on chemical composition, he has an obsession with experimenting with transformation without success. Lucas is the key he has warehouses".

"And access to the chemicals and materials, together you five will work as a team and take part in the divine art of making gold. I want it mass produced then stored in various warehouses for future generations".

"Trust is a must, each member of the team when the gold is mass produced will be entitled to a five percent share, thus the more gold you produce the richer you become. Gold stands for light, wisdom and intelligence; my past experience is that trust is but a lost realm of our bitter imagination. Suspicion is but a lost soul with an ends to a means. Come closer and receive the book from my hand."

They both stand simultaneously; David had an uneasy feeling as he moved forward slowly and fearfully gazing into Cavoc's strange green eyes.

"Come closer don't be frightened, I am trusting you with my priceless book, it will make you rich. Life is but a jigsaw puzzle, look for signs, numbers or letters that spell out your destiny or demise."

David stopped and stood before Cavoc.

"Here you are".

David reached out his hand, nervous fingers shaking with fear as he took hold of the book, all of a sudden Cavoc reached out and spoke.

"Wealth is but a seed, the more it grows the more you greed, the four I have picked out will not let me down or they will suffer eternal damnation in my dimension."

Without warning Cavoc placed his hand on David's shoulder. All of a sudden he felt a burning sensation, he cried out in agony falling to his knees in pain. Cavoc then moved his hand.

"Stand up you are confused".

"Why the unprovoked attack?"

"Well let me explain, you now have the mark of Cavoc upon you. If you do not succeed in your task the burning sensation will spread all over your body, a slow death awaits you."

David was gripped by a flush hot panic attack, he was shaken and dazed. Cavoc's mood all of a sudden changed, as did his nature.

"Good oh I am sorry what came over me. Once the gold is being mass-produced you will return to see me. I will remove the mark. The pain is easing is it not?"

David took a deep breath then raised himself to his feet.

"I see you haven't lost grip of the book that is good."

"Cavoc I am destined to succeed. I have no concept of failure, trust me failure is not an option".

"How will I return once I have succeeded?"

"Good positive thoughts; my friend Nostradamus will contact you. Now I will return you; close your eyes."

David cautiously closed his eyes. Cavoc in a deep powerful voice spoke. "A strange derelict, a feeling of intense warmth then a bright blinding light."

A few minutes later he is back with Nostradame. David opened his eyes. Was it all just a bad dream, horror beyond his imagination?

Nostradame approached.

"David you met up with Cavoc what did he say?"

"He told me you are a kind and wise man"

"Will you require my services in the future? Does Cavoc want you to return?".

"Yes".

"Good until that day I will await your return, let me ask you one question, the book you grip onto so tightly is it a present from Cavoc?"

"Yes."

"May I take a look at it? I have a passion for books?"

"I am sorry Cavoc told me to trust no man."

"Your boots are here let me hold the book whilst you put on your boots."

"No that will not be necessary. I will just place the book on the table".

Nostradame was full of curiosity. Books to Nostradame were spiritual purity and enlightenment. David now complete with boots and his book.

"This way my friend, down the spiral staircase and then out through the door. Until we meet again my friend, goodbye. I hope you can find what you seek".

David smiled, they then parted company. James appeared.

"This way. I see you carry the book Duval and Lucas have joined us. I bet you know already."

"Yes Cavoc told me all about them".

"Good".

They walk along the cobbled streets; people were going about their business. The streets were dark and dirty; the old warehouse on the outskirts of town is where they are going to. They soon arrive. James knocks on the old heavy oak doors five times; the doors remained locked for security, the sounds of the heavy bolts being unlocked and then the door opens. Slowly Mabus appears.

"Come in quickly, this way my friends".

They both enter as David gazes around the dirty damp dark warehouse. In the corner five stacks of lead bars, a bookshelf to the right full of old books in a condition of decay and then a bit further a sinister looking laboratory. A clutter of old jars complete with cobwebs and then a giant furnace. On a table sat leather gloves and aprons, the light was poor. All of a sudden two men appeared, they moved slowly towards David who was glowing with anticipation. The first of the two men introduced himself.

"Hi David I am Duval Wolfe, oh don't look so frightened".

He was a strange looking character so confident his voice was hoarse with suppressed excitement.

"My friend you keep such a tight hold of the book it is time to release your grip. I will translate it. The sooner the better".

David laughed then handed the book to Duval, he opened the book with great anticipation.

"It is written in Hebrew".

The pictures are of a young man; he had wings on his legs.

"I am off now I need peace and quiet to carry on with the translation, I will speak to you later."

It was now the turn of Lucas to speak to David.

"Hello my name is Lucas, it is such an honour to finally meet you. It is you that has made all this possible you are a king amongst men, King David. Once the gold has been mass-produced we all shall be Kings. I will keep supplying and mixing the correct chemicals. I have tried for many years, but the transformation of lead to gold has always eluded me until now. The book Cavoc stole from the Jew is priceless, it has the formula".

David looked into his cold eyes. Lucas was struck with fever, gold fever; his close fitting clothes and craggy face complete with a pointed nose and chin.

"I shall go and consult with Duval".

Mabus approached David with a drink.

"Here my friend you have done us all proud returning with the book."

"Mabus is it really possible to produce gold from lead?"

"Yes if Cavoc says the book has the ancient formula to produce gold, then all we need is Duval to translate it."

David slowly sipped the wine, "It is vintage just like the book".

"Let us now seek out Duval he is a fast reader, this way." They all walk to the end of the warehouse there sitting on an old oak table Duval, James and Lucas waited patiently.

Duval sat reading the book. His eyelids flickering spasmodically. David and Mabus sat on the table; everyone's eyes were turned full upon Duval in complete silence. After five minutes Duval confidently laughed out loud.

"It is all here, five leaves, a king with a broadsword, the sun the moon, an old man; he has open wings, an hour glass on his head and a scythe in his hand as if he were to cut off a young man's feet".

Duval turned the page, a high mountain on its summit, a blue plant with gold leaves and white and red flowers shaking in the wild wind. Griffins and dragons, the snake entwined rod of mercury, messenger of the Gods.

"I must admit the pictures are hard to understand, the writing is in Hebrew. I have translated it. Nigredo, which means putrefaction this is the first stage in the path to creating gold."

Duval complete with jet-black hair and raven coloured eyes stands on his feet and begins to dance.

"Let us celebrate all around".

Happiness was abundant Mabus stands and speaks.

"Wait everyone let us not get carried away, the work will be painstaking. Let us start this day, this minute".

Duval smiles.

"Mabus is right Lucas show me the acids, powders and yellow wax".

They walk towards the laboratory, Mabus looks towards David.

"What can we do to help?"

"We will carry the lead bars over to the furnace ready for putrefaction."

"Good, come on James we have lead to lift."

The three walk over to the lead bars stacked high; slowly they each carry the lead to a space next to the furnace. Duval and Lucas are busy mixing various chemicals; the smell took David's breath away. They both experimented wearing leather aprons and gloves. Duval then speaks.

"Base metal lead oxidises relatively easy and reacts variably with diluted hydrochloric acid. I will put lead into a crucible then into the fire the temperature must be ninety eight degrees."

Lucas then speaks, "I have the eagles wing, a dripping yellow wax. David you and the others this will take a while why not sit down and rest you weary legs. The next process only requires the two of us".

David nods in agreement and the three sit down together. David listen quietly to the conversion between Duval and Lucas, the washing away of all impurities citrinitas the yellowing of the Lunar consciousness; Rubedo the total fusion of spirit and matter. David could see the fumes a cloud of smoke rises into the air and the sound of bubbling and hissing echoes all around the warehouse. The smell of the lead burning in the furnace.

Duval adds various chemicals from old bottles and jars sweat pours from his forehead he then shouts out.

"The work is painstaking but I will succeed, let us leave and return later".

Duval approaches David.

"Cavoc, what did he say?"

"We shall sit and listen to what David has to say."

"Alright my friends, Cavoc believes the key to our success is secrecy. Only us five must know about our experiments, when we go into full production Cavoc wants me to return to his dimension where he will give me final instructions he also informed me that once we have fulfilled our obligation to Cavoc each of us shall have a five per cent share of the gold. He also will not tolerate any treachery. I have witnessed his power first hand if any of us fail we suffer damnation in the fifth dimension".

Lucas looks confused his eyes betrayed by greed.

"The gold that is left, what shall become of it?" His voice shrouded with greed.

"It is no concern of yours, Cavoc will decide what becomes of the gold. I believe next time I visit Cavoc he will provide me with all the answers to your questions."

Duval stands up and speaks, "Let us all go to the table where the wine awaits."

David smiles as they all walk over to the table, pour wine then sit and drink.

Lucas looks over to Duval, "Shall we take a look at the process of the putrefaction?"

"Yes". Duval stands up and they both investigate the process.

James laughs out loud, "This is like some kind of insane fantasy, I cannot believe we are on the verge of producing gold from lead".

Duval returns, "My friends, so far so good, the impurities have been washed away, we have added various chemicals and powders the yellowing of the lunar consciousness has began."

Excitement was the order of the day and they all sat up with anticipation. Lucas returned with good news, "Duval the golden crystals have dissolved, soon we will administer the total fusion of spirit and matter. The colours of the rainbow, its presence will turn the lead into gold. Right I will assist you and the process will soon be fulfilled."

Duval and Lucas return to the furnace David looked to Mabus and speaks. "How much lead do we have altogether?"

"Oh about fifty tonnes".

"Can we purchase more lead from anywhere if needed?"

"Yes Duval has a friend who can supply more lead"

They carry on talking, very soon it is late in the evening Duval walks over to David followed by Lucas, he stops in his tracks. He drew a deep breath.

"We have totally transmuted the lead into the best and finest gold, tomorrow we will make several tests then pronounce the gold genuine."

David smiles a smile of relief.

"Thanks my friend, tonight I will sleep well, tonight a all toast my friends".

Everyone pours a drink of wine from the bottles on the old oak tabled to the writer of the book; Cabal The Jew. Everyone repeats Cabal The Jew and they all laugh and continue to drink, the wine was very strong and starts to take effect. David starts to nod off head resting on the table Mabus stands up.

"Right everyone tomorrow the test then mass production. We have celebrated, now we need to sleep; the room at the end of the warehouse has five beds we shall all sleep here tonight."

Mabus walks over to David and helps him to his feet he puts his arms around David and then helps him to walk to the end of the warehouses. This way they walk through a door, the room was small dark and damp. Mabus helps David into his bed, he fell straight to sleep intoxicated by the strong wine he had consumed plenty of. David's subconscious mind started to visit the fifth dimension. He sat before Cavoc once more, he spoke with his usual dominating voice.

"Your world is full of decadence I have entered your domain and observed and to be honest added to the decay, for me trust is but a distant memory. I have witnessed treachery, treason and greed".

"Throughout the centuries I was there when Judas betrayed Jesus for twenty pieces of silver, you are the chosen one, watch out for treachery, trust only your own instincts do not fail me".

All of a sudden Mabus shakes David.

"Wake up you have been having a nightmare my friend it is morning".

"Oh I dreamt of Cavoc he told me to trust no one." Mabus showed an expression of concern he spoke.

"David be honest is there any of us that you have doubt in the slightest?"

David thinks hard he remembers Lucas, his behaviour and cold eyes and obsession with gold.

"I have also looked into his eyes he has been gripped with gold fever for many years. I Mabus will keep an close eye on Lucas."

All of a sudden Duval appears.

"My friends here is a sample".

Duval hands a gold bar to David the golden shine, the weight and smoothness.

"My god David, I cannot believe the process was so easy, the Jew Cabal he was a genius! It is a work of art; just imagine the gold he produced to keep in favour with the Roman emperors. Cavoc stole the book then the Romans declared war on the Jews, imagine the amount of blood that has been spilt over this book".

David draws a breath then speaks, "The biggest killer of man is religion; Cavoc stole the book for a greater service to mankind, the next time I visit Cavoc he will give me more answers, the sooner the better.

"The answers might help me sleep at night."

David laughs as Duval pulls a funny face. Lucas and James approach and Lucas speaks, "We have started to mass produce, very soon we will all be rich men."

"Oh I like the sight of gold".

David gazed into the eyes of Lucas and beyond; he imagines he could sense a mind ridden with greed. David then turned his mind to the task at hand, weeks of work turned to months and the gold multiplied. Very soon the fifty tonnes of lead became gold. David knew it was about time to visit Cavoc once more.

Duval approached David. "I need to seek out my friend Henry, he has the lead we need".

"Can he deliver without raising any suspicion amongst the authorities."

"Yes he has plenty of lead and is very trustworthy I will leave now and visit him, will you accompany me?"

"No I must visit Cavoc once more".

James suddenly appears with word, "Nostradame will see you straight away, he is in good spirits, he has just received a licence to practise the healing arts."

David hurried with James to the Merchants' House where Nostradame was waiting patiently. James and David left the warehouse and walked along the cobbled streets to the Merchants' House, they soon arrived, the door opened and there stood beaming with confidence, a man of great intelligence Nostradame.

"Come in David, Cavoc awaits your return".

"I believe congratulations are in order, you are now a practising doctor".

"Yes Cavoc has told me your mother died of the Black Death; millions have died since it started in China. Cavoc explained to me the best way to treat victims of the plague. His words of wisdom have helped me save many lives, I owe him a debt of gratitude."

David knew this was the good side of Cavoc. David then spoke his mind, "The plague is such a cruel death, a cure would benefit mankind, there have been too many unfortunate deaths"

"Follow me my friend let us go to my study."

David follows Nostradame up the spiral stairs then into the study.

"David come and look at my book collection."

David gazed at the shelves filled to capacity with books on astrology, mathematics, medicine, Latin and Greek.

"What do you think David? I also have ancient books on magic and the occult, these I keep separate." Nostradame began to shake, "I fear for my safety collecting such books. I risk the tortures of the holy inquisition".

"Do not fear my friend I will not tell anyone".

Nostradame laughed, "I have always sought knowl-edge, Cavoc has helped me. I have started to write down the prophecies he can see in the future, he has told me eventually all of the predictions will make up a great book which will be published in the year a close friend will die.

"Ten years after his death I shall pass away myself Cavoc speaks to me in riddles. Well my friend let us ready you for your journey let us not keep Cavoc waiting any more, over there the bowl of water and the brass stool."

David turned and walked over to the stool, he removed his boots and placed his feet into the cold water that sent a shiver down his spine. Nostradame held his laurel aloft and started to speak the spell that would send David to the fifth dimension.

"Gaze into the water and concentrate as before".

His hands and feet began to shake vigorously but this time he felt slightly composed. a flash of bright light then David found himself back in the fifth dimension, the same strange landscape. David turned and there before him sat Cavoc. He walked towards him; suddenly Cavoc spoke the same seating arrangements. David turned as Cleopatra's throne appeared from nowhere David slowly sat down.

"Right David lets get down to business. Tell me of the gold, is it perfection, if so how much have you produced?"

"Up to now, fifty tonnes. Duval has left to collect more lead."

"Good the more the merrier! Look to your feet David".

David bent over and picked up the strange object. "The pyramid is indestructible and impossible to open, only you or of your bloodline may be permitted to open the pyramid, put your right hand on top and it will open."

David cautiously placed his right hand on top of the pyramid, it opened and David looked inside; five compartments, in each a set of cards and then a golden chain the star of David and then a repulsive sight in the centre of the star; an eye.

"Yes my small sacrifice, the eye of Cavoc. I know you are wondering why; look further into the pyramid."

David reached inside and lifted out a small book he opened the book and Cavoc spoke. "There are various spells and instructions on how the five fives will be conducted. Listen carefully, you will have a son, when he is fifteen you will explain everything about the five fives to him he will do the same with his son and so on. Five generations of your bloodline. Remember I can see into the future, this will take us to the year seventeen hundred and fifty, my dimension will cease to provide good and evil in your domain. The balance of the fifth dimension must be withheld. Good and evil must do battle to withhold the balance Thus the keeper of the five fives will arrange for five twenty-five year olds to pass over to the fifth dimension, there they will battle for the ultimate prize; the chance to be the new keeper, all of the riches so shall they inherit twenty five years later again five more will do battle and so on until the end of your world.

"The cards Cavoc what are they for?"

"Yes I was coming around to them, the first card is dealt the place of battle for example a field or maybe a swamp. The next a weapon, a spear or sword and then help an angel or saint. The next foe; a beast or snake and then the fate is decided. The secret order of the five fives will carry on throughout the centuries; long after you have departed from your realm, secrecy is the key to eternity. Mankind will start to embrace new technology; in centuries to come mankind will have access to weapons of mass destruction.

"Nostradamus, he is always seeking answers, he seeks knowledge of future events. I told him of a great war that would stretch across all continents. I did not tell him the whole truth, but it was too far fetched even for him to understand. The persecution of the Jews started when I took the book off Cabal. A demon by the name of Dogon, spelt backwards my friend, no God; his disciples even now have a deep hatred of the Jew they spread the word. Jews are responsible for the Black Death, thousands are still being slaughtered. Later in the nineteenth century Dogon will be reborn and will be responsible for a war that will kill millions upon millions. His name will be Hisler I have told Nostradamus Hisler. It could be Hitler, his followers brought Dogon back, using the book of dead their ultimate goal is mass extermination of the Jewish people. His evil will know no bounds and he will try to gain total control of the world. He will tell the people of Germany that he will lead their mighty country back to her rightful glory.

"The die would be cast; possessed by a demon, Hitler will change from a shy timid speaker to the most powerful, spellbinding orator, he will be able to weave a spell binding effect over his audience, his eyes and voice filled with supernatural power and hatred he will reap sadistic vengeance on the Jew. He will study books on ancient Rome and occult practices, the German people will become zombified servants until they are liberated from the spell by an allied victory.

"The war will last for six years, six million Jews will be exterminated, the total loss of life will be sixty million The three sixes the sign of the beast, the darkest chapter of human history. Dogon once again will be killed and sent back to hell, his disciples of mass murder some disappeared others hunted down like dogs. The Jews will extract revenge. Oh how history repeats itself. the reason I have told you all of this is Dogon's disciples made a pact with him before he died. The book and any gold produced would be his again when he was to be reborn".

David listened to Cavoc he then spoke, "I have listened to your words, Dogon must not be reborn; what if I was to seek out his corpse and cremate it in this century.

Cavoc smiled, "What a noble idea, but quite impossible his body is well hidden and well guarded it would be suicide for anyone to undertake such a task I am afraid the future cannot be altered"

"His disciples could be anywhere."

"Is there anyone you do not trust?"

"One hundred per cent think David I must know Lucas he suffers from gold fever he lusts for what he cannot have, you and Lucas will take the gold to secret locations only you and Lucas. His father was a very good businessman before he died of the plague. Storage was his business he owned five warehouses in various locations, Lucas knows where they were, as his Father left them to him go with Lucas and deliver the gold. Offer him an increase to his cut, if necessary to buy the warehouses off him. I will set up a secret society of the five fives it will flourish until the end of time, the gold will be invested into property in the new world of liberty, the last visit to the fifth dimension will occur in the year two thousand twenty-five years. Later the world will end. Nostradamus will have his book published in the month of March in Lyons in fifteen fifty-five. This is five fives is it not. I have blessed him with divine knowledge, a series of prophecies though out the centuries, I have provided him with prophecies until the end of the world. Nostradamus does not know of this, he consults the stars for his own answers.

"Before the end of the world I believe a writer with the gift will put pen to paper, remember there is no greater power than the written word, he will share the same Christian name as you. Remember numbers will play a great part in his life he will study numerology as I did in the fifth century with an old friend the philosopher Pythagoras. He believed numbers are the essence of life. Numerology is as old as time, my domain is the fifth dimension. I surround myself in the good and the evil of the five fives. Numbers David, imagine the year two thousand and twenty-five, add up the first numbers twenty and twenty-five."

David listened to Cavoc mesmerised by his words then spoke. "Four and five add them together you get nine place the nine and five transform the numbers into the alphabet what does it spell out for your domain?"

"Your world is going to die".

David could sense Cavoc's words radiating with more and more power.

"I will now tell you the five possible endings; The first China. Over a fifth of the population speaks Chinese, as China represents a full twenty percent of the world's population, so one in every five people on the planet is a resident of China. Three million troops. Nostradamus believes it to be two million. The countries of Europe and the new country suffer great depression and they all completely cut back on their weapons and armies, whilst China becomes the greatest super power of all time.

"They will produce five new advanced aircraft carriers complete with radar evading fighter jets. New types of missiles. China secretly becomes the most powerful out of the five nuclear powers recognised by a treaty. China produces a multi-megaton missile they call it Nukia they produce enough missiles to wipe out the new country. The plan will start in nineteen ninety-five, China will send five thousand suicide sleepers to the new country to unleash hell on the chosen day along with thousands of China's elite blue team cyber attackers; the plan is simple.

"Attack the infrastructure and nuclear bases without warning. It would be completely nuked. Russia and North Korea would then step in with China and then Europe would be at the mercy of the two great super powers. The fight will continue until the mass destruction causes the end of the world. The next is my favourite as I have observed them throughout the centuries from a distance; the alien.

"Moses spoke to me on the subject he believed as I do the alien would one day invade earth. They have visited earth since the dawn of time; they have experimented on humans for centuries looking for a super bug that could wipe out the human race without the devastation. The earth would be remade to suit the aliens needs by two thousand and twenty-five. A hundred new planets are discovered the leader of the alien assault team Akkas deploys five heavy bombers full of biological weapons, they release the bombs on the countries that they believe are the super powers, the bombs cause limited damage but the germs once released and inhaled cause all of the bodies vital organs to stop resulting in death in less than five minutes. Afterwards the invasion would start, resulting in the death of all life of earth, the next of the five is the virus your mother died of; the black death, along with twenty million others the new virus attacks the brain turning humans into wild animals".

"A certain hunger for flesh, man's greatest fear the carnivorous virus also causes zombie like behaviour, mass suicide, mass riots and a complete meltdown of the human race. The fourth the ozone, the collapse of the ozone layer, the ultra violet UV radiation strong enough to cause sunburn in five minutes, DNA mutating UV radiation is up five hundred percent harmful effects to the planets animals and skin cancer, cataracts and immune system damage. Most of the world suffering from a lack of water, the seas turn to acid, crops fail, billions die of starvation and the rest of the human race fight each other for survival. Asthma and lung diseases become the biggest killers, a slow death for the human race and last of all; the great king of terror comes from the sky in the shape of a giant comet fifty miles in diameter, the comets name is swift and it will hit the earth with the force of five hundred million hydrogen bombs earth will cease to exist. And there you have the five; China, Alien, Virus, Ozone and Comet. Take each of the first letters what does it spell out?"

David looks to Cavoc in amazement.

"The letters spell out your name Cavoc".

"Correct, one of the five will destroy the human race which one is anyone's guess, mankind does not know that the future is fixed by forces utterly outside their control".

"I realise a lot of what I have said is beyond your comprehension, from now on my only contract with you will be in the land of dreams Nostradamus has fulfilled his task his destiny lies else where".

"The mark on my shoulder, you said you would remove it so I learnt a lesson in trust."

"The mark of Cavoc will never spread but it will remain like a tattoo, a reminder never lower your guard."

David had turned extremely pale, who could he trust, Cavoc had lied to him. David stood up with great hesitation he then spoke.

"I have the pyramid, send me back to my domain."

"Alright David, I had a change of heart move closer and I will remove the mark." David moved closer and Cavoc placed his hand on David's shoulder, a cold sensation then Cavoc cast a healing spell.

"The mark is now gone, it will not return as you came full of happiness close your eyes".

Cavoc spoke a strange dialect as David stood completely still again, his mind paralysed by Cavoc's strange spell the warmth then the light. David was soon back with Nostradame.

"Welcome my friend you have been gone a while Nostradame watched with fixed fascination as David placed the pyramid on the table then proceeded to put on his boots".

"Another present Cavoc honours you."

"What is it a pyramid?"

Nostradame's inquisitive nature was all so clear. "I am sworn to secrecy my friend".

"Oh well one question before you leave, has Cavoc mentioned when the world will end?"

David laughs then speaks. "My friend the world will never end, Nostradamus looked to David in disbelief he then spoke, "I am leaving tomorrow, seeking out the sick and healing them. One more thing before you go, I believe you would not be here before me if it was not for Mabus, he uses dark forces, always be on your guard whilst around him."

"Thank you Nostradamus I will keep an eye on him, but I believe he would never betray Cavoc. Until we meet again my friend".

"That's strange how did you know I have changed my name to Nostradamus? Oh Cavoc told you, farewell my friend".

David walked down the spiral stairs and through the door holding the pyramid. James was outside sitting down on a step.

"My you have been a while, Cavoc had a lot to say, the pyramid, what's inside it?"

"Its a long story I will tell you another time" They walked together along the cobbled road back to the warehouse surrounded by shadows.

Soon they arrived back at the warehouse and James knocked on the door five times, a brief silence and then Mabus opened the door and they both entered. David then spoke to Mabus.

"Is everything alright has the lead arrived?"

"No Duval has yet to return, the box you carry what is inside it?"

"Oh its a present from Cavoc where is Lucas? I need to speak with him".

"He is checking the quality of the gold again David, put the pyramid in a safe place first then sort out Lucas. David approached Lucas.

"Hi David, the quality of the gold is amazing"

David watched as Lucas picked up the gold his eyes lit up like a candle, his fingers twitching, lost in a trance like state David spoke completely unnerved, "We must pack the gold bars into wooden boxes and transport them to hidden locations.

"Good, are the others to know of the locations?"

"No, good you obviously trust me and not the other three. Cavoc told me about your departed father, he was in the business of storage and owned five warehouses"

"Yes I still have the keys Cavoc, wants me to buy them off you. Naturally your cut of the gold will increase to ten percent"

"Cavoc is most generous and well informed. Yes let me think make it fifteen percent and we have a deal?"

With great hesitation David agreed, he remembered Cavoc's words there is method in my madness.

"Shall I tell the others?"

"No it will be our secret".

"Good David, jealousy can be man's greatest evil now let us fill the crates with gold".

They started to begin to fill the crates all of a sudden James and Mabus appeared James spoke, "Can we help?"

"Yes the gold must be boxed up and moved to secret locations by order of Cavoc".

Mabus showed bitter disappointment, blinking and frowning then like a flash of lightening he expressed annoyance.

"Are you moving all the gold, what happens if Duval does not return?"

David gazed into his cold eyes then spoke, "Calm yourself we will leave some gold here for you to guard no one will be cheated out of their share that I promise all of you".

Utter silence then Mabus spoke, "I am sorry I don't know what came over me".

Lucas whispered to David, "sounds like gold fever to me".

David looked in total disbelief then spoke, "Let us all start to load as many crates as possible".

They all started to load up the wagon very soon the wagon was loaded. David looked to Mabus and said, "Can you and James collect the horses from the stables?"

"Yes".

Mabus opened the large oak doors it was dark, Mabus and James collected the horses then attached them to the wagon.

"Right Lucas the time is right for us to leave. Mabus I will leave you in charge, soon Duval will return you know what to do produce more gold for us". Mabus forced a smile then Lucas cracked his whip and the horses took flight out of the warehouse and into the darkness. David looked to Lucas and spoke.

"Take us to the closest warehouse under the cover of darkness".

They travelled to each warehouse placing ten crates of gold into each and then leaving for the next destination, very soon they were both exhausted. David gazed up at the radiance of the crimson moon and took a deep breath of the damp night air. After several hours of work their task was complete, they locked the lock on the last warehouse David looked to Lucas and spoke, "The keys our deal my friend its not that I don't trust you".

"David this is how it is going to work you shall have four keys the fifth will remain with me until I receive fifteen percent of the gold as we agreed".

David was tired and not in the mood for confrontation he just nodded in agreement. Lucas then handed him the four keys, David placed them in his pocket. He remembered the pyramid, it was indestructible and only he could open it as soon as he got back that would be the safest place for the four keys.

"Lucas, it is starting to get light, we must now return to Montpellier".

They both climbed onto the wagon and in great haste they returned to the warehouse. David yawned, his eyes closing. Lucas brought the wagon to a halt. He then turned his attention to his sleeping friend, "David wake up we are back at the warehouse".

Lucas spoke again and then helped David down from the wagon; he assisted him to the door slowly knocking five times. Mabus opened the door after a brief delay he looked at David.

"What is wrong with him he looks completely exhausted?"

"Yes Mabus help me get him into bed a good sleep will soon cure him".

Mabus assisted Lucas and very soon they had David tucked up in bed, five minutes later another knock on the door it was Duval with the lead. James and Mabus helped him transfer the lead into the warehouse. Whilst Lucas also fell asleep in his bed five hours later David heard the sound of laughter he opened his eyes it was Duval.

He began to talk fluently with a heightened voice, "My friend I have returned with the lead, it is all unloaded and we have started full production once more. The place I have just come from the Protestants are being slaughtered by Catholics in the name of religion. I believe man has always sought out a reason to show the evil that lies dormant in most of us".

"I agree Duval there is too much evil in the world and not enough good".

Lucas climbed out of his bed, his mind wondered back to the promise David had made, fifteen percent of the gold was to be his. Duval left the room and then Lucas seized the opportunity he spoke in a low calm voice.

"My friend there is someone I would like you to meet."

"Who Lucas?"

"My beautiful sister Bella she is such an excellent cook her food is truly delicious".

"David what you need is a good meal inside you". David accepted the dinner invitation.

"Come on David let us waste no more time I will take you to meet her now, do not worry she knows you are coming it is all arranged".

David hesitated for a brief second he remembered the promise he made to Lucas, if the others found out he would feel such wrath David put on his best clothes he splashed some water onto his face. "All right Lucas I am ready, show me to my dinner".

David and Lucas left, informing Duval of their plans on the way out. David inhaled the damp moist air as he gazed up at the radiant sun. Lucas showed David to his sister's dwelling house they entered. David did not know what to expect, apprehensively he entered the dwelling. All of a sudden he heard the voice of an angel she spoke.

"Hello you must be David".

His eyes turned full upon her he was quite taken back by her beauty the fineness of her features, slim blonde in her early twenties complete with the face of an angel. Lucas laughed out loud, my sister has left you speechless she has that effect on mankind. David stood with a look of total disbelief and then summoned up the courage to speak.

"Bella what can I say you're beautiful such a comfort to the eye".

He was mesmerised and moved determinedly towards the angel.

"Thank you sir my brother has told me so much about your intelligence, honesty, good looks complete with a heart of gold"

David laughed to himself he could smell her sweet scents he took a deep breath enchanted by her engaging smile.

"Bella your fragrance is quite divine".

Lucas knew that David was completely snared by his beautiful sister and left quietly through the door.

"David walk with me into the dinning area, I promised my brother I would cook you a special meal. My late mother Rosie was such an excellent cook">

David gazed at Bella, she looked infinitely attractive, beauty beyond his wildest dreams, they enter the dinning room. Hanging from the walls were detailed colourful paintings and in the centre of the room a large Gothic engraved dark oak table with matching chairs. The table is set for two, in the centre of the table sat a vase containing five red roses. Fine silver cutlery and two silver candelabras all placed to perfection. Bella spoke slowly her sparkling smile such a delicate looking woman.

"David this your seat".

"Thank you Bella".

David sat with his eyes fixed on Bella.

"David this is a small guesthouse it is owned by my late mothers aunty her name is Donna, she is helping me in the kitchen."

All of a sudden a pleasant old lady appeared, in her hand a silver tray complete with two drinking vessels and a vintage bottle of wine. Her face was of cool ivory.

"Right Bella be seated, everything is ready. Bella I shall wait on you for a change, this stunning young man must be David".

"Thank you it's a pleasure to meet you kind lady".

Donna smiled in appreciation of David's charm, Bella sat down thanking Donna.

David gazed at the red roses; they seemed to radiate an atmosphere of love. Donna poured the wine and then returned to the kitchen Bella looked to David.

"Isn't she such a sweet old lady".

David agreed nodding his head. Donna then reappeared in her hands a large silver tray.

"Here we are my little lovebirds, dinner is served. Memories of his dear departed mother came flooding back as he inhaled the aroma of the cooked lamb. Donna placed the tray on the table before carving the lamb. Very soon placed in front of the two were plates filled with lamb and various vegetables.

Donna smiled. "Now for the sauce". She spoke ever so quietly. "Its a secret recipe handed down through the generations".

She poured the sauce onto the lamb, David looked at the hearty meal with real excitement, he then turned to Donna and spoke. "Thank you this looks delicious".

David picked up his knife and fork and began to eat his dinner, the meal met with his approval. His taste buds were truly in heaven. Donna smiled and then returned to the kitchen leaving David and Bella to enjoy each other's company, very soon their plates where empty. Bella gazed into David's eyes, she took a deep breath and spoke to David.

"I don't want you to be cross with my brother Lucas but he has told me all about the gold.

"Lucas and I are very close, he looked after me after our parents died of the plague. I don't know what I would do if anything were to happen to him".

David looked to Bella confused then said. "Trust me my fair maiden nothing will happen to your brother, as for the gold I completely have faith in you not to tell anyone else".

All of a sudden the sweet sound of music could be heard from outside, a violinist was playing. Bella closed her eyes and then reopened them. Her eyes sparkled with desire, she stood up, her blue satin dress matched her eyes. She looked to David.

"Come closer and take my hand, let us dance".

David got to his feet mesmerised by her delicately drawn features, his eyes turned full upon her and he moved closer and took hold of her delicate hand. They danced and drew closer and closer, he saw curiosity in her eyes she began to stroke his hair, next she kissed him passionately on the lips. All of a sudden a knock on the door they both regained their composure as the door then opened it was Lucas a face of horror and pure panic. Bella rushed over to find out what was wrong. Lucas cried out.

"A messenger has arrived bearing bad news my son Claude was attacked in the forest by a beast. He is badly injured, later the beast was tracked down and killed the messenger informed me he is with fever and is asking for me. I must leave for his village immediately it is but a forty mile ride".

David looked to Lucas, he had a bad feeling something wasn't right. Lucas kissed his sister on the cheek and then rushed off into the night. David looked to Bella, her eyes began to glisten with tears. David embraced holding her tight and then he kissed her on the cheek. He then spoke with a reassuring voice.

"Do not worry, do not shed tears on such a pretty face, your brother shall return safely'.

David wiped away the tears from her delicate cheeks.

"Bella I must go now and inform the others of this situation I shall return tomorrow if that is alright".

Bella smiled and kissed David. "I shall see you tomorrow my fair prince".

Once more he looked to her face of transcendent beauty. "Good night my princess give my gratitude to Rosie, this has been the best day of my life until tomorrow".

His voice echoed with happiness he then turned and left the guesthouse, returning to the warehouse. In front of the large oak door stood a tall dark figure it was Mabus. He looked at David, a glare of disapproval, he then spoke in his usual cold-hearted manner

"You have been out enjoying yourself with the sister of Lucas leaving all the work to us".

David became angry, "Have you forgotten yourself Mabus, if you are not happy then leave I will contact Cavoc and have you replaced".

He spoke knowing it was about time Mabus was put in his place Mabus shook his head, the door suddenly opened it was Duval he looked at Mabus.

"David what is going on I overheard the conversation we must not argue or fall out. Mabus you are wrong without David none of this would have been possible, remember this before you speak. If David wants to enjoy himself then let him be. I know once all the gold is produced I shall be doing the same".

Duval smiled, "By the way where is Lucas?"

David took a deep breath, "Lucas has left to visit his son he was attacked by a beast in the forest".

Mabus looked at David, his face bore a cold-hearted smile, before David could react Mabus disappeared into the shadows. David and Duval entered the warehouse closing the door behind them; Duval put his arm around David, he yawned.

"You have a sense for these things, do you think Lucas will be alright?"

"Yes Duval, it is late I need my beauty sleep".

"You could say that again".

They both laughed then made their way to their beds David got into bed and said goodnight. As soon as his head hit the pillow he was in a deep sleep, he dreamt he was watching a mysterious horse rider galloping along a dark dirt path. David looks to the riders face bleary-eyed, pale, a face of pure fear, he suddenly recognised the face of the horseman. It was Lucas; a full moon shone down, a cool breeze left trees and shrubs moving to and fro. All of a sudden David could hear scurrying amongst the leaves. David shivered through his body as he heard the howl of the wolf. David watched in horror as a pack of wolves attacked, the supernatural beasts leaped from all sides of the forest.

Poor Lucas never stood a chance, his horse bolted throwing him to the ground at the mercy of the wild-eyed wolves, his cries and screams echoed around the dark forest as the beasts ripped him to pieces. David opened his eyes in shock, he gazed around at shadows, was this a bad dream or a cruel vision of the demise of Lucas. He lay with his eyes open until daybreak. David climbed out of bed and walked over to the table pouring himself a drink. One by one Duval and James got out of their beds. Duval approached David and spoke.

"Mabus never returned, probably drowning his sorrows all night".

David became distressed he remembered the nightmare. Duval looked to David, "What is the matter?"

David shook his head, "Its Lucas I dreamt he was attacked and killed by a pack of wolves on the way to the village, what shall I tell his sister Bella?"

Duval looked into David's eyes and smiled.

"My friend you tell her nothing, forget all about your nightmare everyone has them". David shook his head he then spoke.

"You're right what was I thinking of, it was nothing more than a bad dream, but so vivid I was there watching but unable to do anything".

Duval smiled then turned to James. "Is it alright if David visits his lady friend whilst we produce more gold?"

James nodded his head in agreement, "Good. David you may visit your princess with our blessings".

Duval laughed, "Go on my friend your angel awaits".

David thanked the both of them. A change of clothes, a quick wash and he was on his way. He opened the door and looked to the ground as rays of light shone into his eyes, he turned and closed the door and then made his way towards the guesthouse, as he got closer he saw Bella sitting on the steps of the guesthouse. Moisture shone all over her face, her eyes glittered in the radiant glory of the sun. David looked at Bella sitting with a sad face, in her hands a bunch of freshly picked flowers. Bella stood up and whispered to David.

"My parents died on this day ten years ago. I must visit the graveyard and pay my respects, would you like to accompany me my prince".

David whispered back to Bella, "Why it would be an honour to accompany you my fair maiden".

"Good take my hand and I shall lead the way".

Hand in hand they walked along the cobbled streets towards the graveyard.

It was a mid-summers day, the radiant sun shone onto her golden hair. It was quiet and peaceful people minding their own business. An old man hobbling along the cobbled streets spoke.

"Bonjour Monsieur".

And fair maiden Bella returned the complement. Very soon they were crossing the old wooden bridge, Bella stopped and gazed beneath the bridge. The sound of running water, such a relaxing sound in these dark times, romance was not quite dead. Bella lifted her head and began to gaze upwards, at clouds sailing across the sky, she closed her eyes her straight blonde hair hung around her face and shoulders. David moved closer swiftly without noise began caressing and kissing her. David gazed into her open light blue eyes and spoke of his love, passionately kissing Bella again and again. She smiled such an engaging smile.

"Come on David we must not keep my parents waiting any longer".

David smiled as then crossed a field to the graveyard; memories of his own departed parents came flooding back to David. His mother died of the plague his father murdered at the hands of paid assassins. Suddenly Bella stopped at a grave whispering a short player, then knelt and placed the flowers next to the gravestone. As she stood a single tear ran down her angelic face, David placed his arm around Bella as she wiped away her tears. Bella looked up into David's eyes and regained her composure. She spoke softly, "I believe in destiny our love was meant to be". She casually kissed David's cheek and lips.

"My prince I am truly famished, will you return with me to the guesthouse as early on I prepared some mutton broth".

David smiled, "Yes I to am truly famished".

David held her hand as they returned to the guesthouse when they arrived Rosie appeared in the doorway she laughed the spoke with a heightened voice.

"Why it's the two lovebirds hand-in-hand, come in the table is set".

Bella smiled then thanked Rosie and they entered the guesthouse, going into the dinning area. Rosie poured them a drink as they sat down, Rosie then whispered to Bella.

"You both having the mutton broth?"

Bella nodded David sat gazing into Bella's blue eyes, very soon Rosie returned with the broth, she placed it on the table and then there was a loud bang on the door. Rosie answered the door it was Duval.

Rosie called to David, "It is your friend Duval he has a message for you. David looked at Bella.

"Will you excuse me for a minute my dear". David stood up and walked over to Duval. "What is a matter?"

Duval shook his head, "My friend Lucas he never made it to the village". A draught of cold air suddenly ran down David's spine, Duval continued the story.

"The villagers found what was left of his horse, the village elder recognised the saddle as it had his late fathers crest on it. All that was left of Lucas was blood and ripped clothing".

David remembered his nightmare he then wondered how he would tell Bella the tragic news. Duval shook his head once more, he remembered his sister and several children simply disappeared he then began to tell David the story.

"My late father and a dozen hunters caught a man who lived in the forest, his name was Modus he killed the children, my sister was one of his victims. My father found her partially eaten body. He and the hunters were so sickened by what they found they beat him then hanged him from a tree, to make sure he was dead they cut him down and decapitated him, setting fire to what was left of his body. Evil forces were at work, werewolves the whole of France is gripped by attacks from these beasts".

David remembered Cavoc's words the beasts were crossing over from his dimension reaping havoc in this domain. David regained his composure then spoke quietly.

"I will inform Bella of her brothers disappearance".

Duval put a brave face on then returned to the warehouse, David returned to Bella her face reflecting a shade of terror then anger.

"What has happened to my brother he told me he feared betrayal, he mentioned his share of the gold tell me what has happened to him?"

David stood next to Bella. "I am sorry your brother has disappeared, he never made it to the village, they found his horse".

"So why has it not been returned to me".

David hesitated taking a deep breath. "I am sorry the horse was found dead".

Bella stood frozen motionless with a contorted distraught face, full of tears. David embraced her tenderly; he felt some how he was to blame even though he had no control over Cavoc's beasts.

All of a sudden Rosie appeared with a puzzled face. "Whatever is the matter my dear I could hear crying its your brother isn't it? What has happened to him?"

Rosie looked to David, "I over heard your friend mention wolves".

Her voice then turned to anger, "Them dam wolves they should shoot the lot of them".

Bella turned pale then fainted; David kept hold of her Donna spoke in a calm voice. "It's the shock of it all, follow me. David lets get her to her bed, the poor girl needs rest".

David picked up Bella and carried her to her bedroom gently placing her on the bed, Donna put on a brave face.

"I shall nurse Bella I want you to stay in the guestroom across the corridor, that way if I need you I can give you a call is that alright dear?"

"Yes thank you Donna, here it will soon be dark, take this candle".

Donna lit the candle and then handed it to David, "You look a bit tired yourself try and get a good nights sleep I promise Bella will be a lot better tomorrow".

David smiled, he held the candle in front of him as he left the room and walked across the corridor. It was now starting to get dark, he opened the door. Inside the atmosphere was damp. He closed the door behind him placing the candle on a small table. David removed his boots the cold floorboards creaked as he walked towards the bed. He was surrounded by shadows as he climbed into bed he could hear the sound of rats scratching in the room above. Suddenly rain started to patter against the window and then the howl of the wind followed by a flash of lightning. David pulled the covers over his head falling into a deep sleep. He dreamt of everything that had happened that day he then mumbled in his sleep. "Cavoc where are you?"

All of a sudden Cavoc appeared in David's dream, a dominating voice spoke out. "I know why you seek me out in the land of dreams, the disappearance of Lucas. You must be very upset; I believe you are befriending his sister. I have no inclination to trifle with your happiness, I told you many moons ago that Lucas was not to be trusted, do not comprehend my motives".

David took a deep breath then spoke, "Was it necessary to feed Lucas to your beasts?"

Cavoc laughed out loud then spoke abruptly.

"You slander me, the beasts live in the forest and to ride through it in total darkness on a full moon was not only foolhardy but fatal. I speak the truth if he had waited to daylight before he made the journey he would still be alive today, his death was self inflicted not of my hand".

David spoke out, "Cavoc the beasts are from your dimension thus you have to take responsibility".

"Let me tell you something, the dark forces in your domain that unite with beasts will be tolerated until mankind destroys all evil. The beasts will return to my domain or be wiped off the face of earth".

David gazed into Cavoc's eyes deep down he knew he was telling the truth David spoke up once more.

"What of his share of the gold?" Cavoc smiles and then answers in a low voice. His share, what share? He is no longer of this earth, tomorrow a new replacement will arrive his name is Mason, he is a wealthy business-man who has influence with various authorities. He will help with the building of a rich business empire, ready for the centuries ahead".

Cavoc then slowly began to fade, David opened his eyes and Cavoc was gone, his thoughts switched from Cavoc to Bella it was now morning. He jumped out of bed quickly sliding his feet into his boots, he opened the door and to his amazement there stood before him was Bella, she smiled then hurried towards him, he stepped forward and affectionately embraced her.

"I am sorry about your Brother".

"David there is nothing anyone could have done for my brother, he was foolhardy going into the forest at nightfall and a full moon, if he had waited till daybreak the wolves would not have attacked him. I want you to go now and carry on with your work and I shall see you later".

She kissed David and then he returned to the warehouse. Duval was standing outside the warehouse talking to a mysterious stranger, as he approached them Duval turned and in a loud voice he said. "David this is Mason he will exchange our gold for money".

David answered confidently, "Yes I already know, Cavoc has told me all about Mason a wealthy businessman with connections".

Mason smiled. He was a large man, he wore dark tight fitting clothes, a face of ivory complete with a dark beard his voice was deep and gravely.

"Hello David let us go inside we have much to discuss".

David looked into Mason's eyes he knew he could trust him. "This way my friend we need to talk in private".

They entered the warehouse, once inside Mabus appeared from the shadows. He stood before David in his usual deep voice he spoke. "Can I speak to you it will take but minutes of your precious time?"

David asked Duval to show Mason to the storage room whilst he spoke with Mabus. David looked into his cold eyes. "What do you want to talk about?"

Mabus took a deep angry breath, "I have had enough, how much more gold will we produce before I get my share I have places I need to be, well away from this stinking warehouse?"

David shook his head, "Mabus patience is a virtue, so I am led to believe".

Mabus gritted his teeth, "My patience young man is wearing thin".

David smiles, "Your right Mabus, you're not getting any younger. You mock me, one day it will be me doing the mocking and you crying out for mercy".

David gazed into his cruel cold raven coloured eyes. Mabus was becoming more and more uncompromising.

David took a deep breath and then spoke with great courage. "Listen Mabus do you want to provoke the wrath of Cavoc, we will all get our share of the gold when Cavoc says so not before".

Mabus shook his head with impatience livid eyes and a dark expression of evil. "So you will not change your mind is this your final word?"

"Yes Mabus this is my final word on the matter".

"I Mabus will not enter the warehouse, my work is done. I will wait for my share in the old tavern you speak to Cavoc weeks, months, I will learn to be patient as long as I get my share".

Mabus then turned and made his way towards the room he had rented out in the tavern. David had a bad feeling Mabus was becoming more and more dangerous. David entered the warehouse closing the door behind him he then discussed business with Mason some of the gold would be used to purchase property in France and other key countries when the business was done David said farewell to Mason then met up with Duval.

"I am sorry my friend Mabus will not be returning he awaits in the old tavern for his share of the gold".

Duval shook his head in disgust, "Can we trust Mabus he has a dark side. I believe this has grown with the production of the gold".

"Duval my first priority is the gold. I shall sleep here tonight Let us produce more gold".

"James has started production good lets go and help him produce more".

They both help working hard for hours, more and more gold is produced. David yawned; closing his eyes for a brief second he then looked to Duval and James.

"We have produced enough gold, let us turn in now we all need our sleep".

Duval smiled, "Are you sure you want to sleep here what about your pretty angel?"

"Oh I will visit her in the morning". Duval nods his head and very soon they are all in their beds fast asleep. Morning soon came around. David opens his eyes and gets out of bed quickly, dressing in clean clothes David left the warehouse and walked over to the guesthouse his mind plagued with thoughts of what Mabus had last said to him. David looked to the door of the guesthouse it was wide open something wasn't right.

David rushed inside and to his horror in front of him was Bella tied to a chair and gagged in the corner of the room on the floor lay the lifeless body of Donna. David rushed over to Bella removing the gag and the bonds, which held her. Bella became hysterical and cried out.

"What has happened?"

"It was Mabus, it was Mabus, he was like a man possessed he attacked poor Donna snapping her neck like a twig he then pulled out a knife and threatened to cut me up into little pieces unless I gave him the key to the gold. I feared for my life. His face was demonic his eyes cold as death. He had two men with him".

"Come with me Bella, we must tell Duval and James".

"What about Donna? I cannot leave her, she died such a cruel death".

"Do not worry James will seek out the priest, she will be in safe hands".

They both left David ran towards the warehouse filled with anger. He banged on the door five times. Duval opened the door gazing into panic stricken eyes.

"What has happened? Calm yourself; tell me what has happened?"

"It's Mabus he has betrayed us, killing Donna and stealing some of the gold".

Duval shook his head, "His evil has no bounds we must find him".

David looked to James, "Can you seek out the priest poor Donna lies dead on a cold floor".

James agreed and left straight away; Duval closed his eyes for a second. "The old tavern Mabus has a room there, let us leave this minute".

David took a deep breath as they left, locking the door behind them. When they arrived at the old tavern David explained to Boris, the owner, about the recent events.

Boris shook his head in disbelief, "I will show you his room; this way".

They all walk up the stairs Boris opens the door to the room, inside evidence of Devil worship. A book on the occult and on the walls strange symbols of the dark arts. Duval finds a letter.

David he read it out slowly, "I planned for months on ways to steal the gold, you left me no choice, you should have given me my share of the gold when I asked for it and Donna would still be alive. Bella only lives because one day she might come in useful. The rest of the gold will be mine. As you are reading this letter I will be on a ship back to England.

"If you try to follow me you will die a slow death. I promise you our paths will cross in the future and you will suffer".

David finished reading out the letter and then after an anxious silence David ripped the letter up in a fit of anger.

"Duval I will consult Cavoc on the best coarse of action to be taken".

Boris looked to David, "You mentioned gold, lots of gold".

David gazed into his eyes, the atmosphere was cold he grew furious he then spoke in a raised voice.

"You must not mention to anybody what has been said here, it secret do I make myself clear?"

Boris grinned, "I understand my friend, secrecy is the key to a long life".

David smiled at Duval. "Let us get back to Bella and James".

They said farewell to Boris and made their way to the guesthouse. As they moved closer and closer they could see the removal of Donna's dead body. In the doorway stood Bella and James. David was filled with anger and sorrow; he moved swiftly towards Bella he gazed at her contorted distraught face, full of tears, he embraced her.

"Bella calm down, let me wipe away your tears, I am sorry".

"First Lucas now Donna, who will be next?"

"There won't be a next, Mabus has fled with the gold to England hopefully we will never see him again".

David turned and spoke to Duval, "You and James return to the warehouse I shall stay with Bella".

Duval nods in approval then returns to the warehouse with James, Bella wipes away her tears.

"It has been such a long day I feel so tired will you escort me to my bed chamber?"

David smiles, "Why certainly my Princess".

Bella forces a smile and hand-in-hand they make their way to the bedroom. Bella opens the door and as they enter Bella turns to David, she is filled with strange emotions.

"Before I sleep I will say a prayer for us both, you are all I have left in this world".

David was speechless, his heart was truly touched, her eyes glittered he was mesmerised by her natural beauty. David embraced her; he kissed her passionately on the cheek and lips. Bella flung herself onto the bed pulling David on top of her; very soon they were lost in each other's arms. Bella's eyes sparkled with desire radiating an atmosphere of love as she ran her fingers through his hair they continued to make love until the early hours.

The following day David awoke, he gazed at Bella such freshness smooth cheeks, her ice blue eyes were open she possessed such appealing beauty David drew a deep breath then kissed her tenderly. Her captivating face grinned broadly, "David, I love you".

He smiled; outside he could hear the whistle of the birds the radiant blazing sunlight shone through the window.

All of this radiated a deep sense of peace, he gathered his thoughts and after a brief hesitation he looked to Bella and said, "I want us to be together forever".

His heart was pounding Bella smiled, "Does this mean we are to be married?"

"Yes my love as soon as my business here is finished would you like to come away with me to Paris?"

"Yes David this place holds to many bad memories".

"Your right we both need a change I will consult my business partners and maybe come up with a brief idea of when the gold will be finished".

"Yes David, kiss me once more".

David kissed Bella tenderly, he then got dressed and made his way to the warehouse, he soon arrived knocking on the door, which Duval opened door with great haste.

"David my friend is everything alright with Bella?"

"Yes Duval I need to contact Cavoc. I must tell him about the circumstances behind the theft of the gold".

Duval looked at David and a draught of cold air suddenly ran down his spine.

"Cavoc's anger will erupt like a volcano, rather you than me my friend."

"Do not worry Duval his wrath will be directed towards Mabus, it is him who has betrayed Cavoc".

David then turned and proceeded towards the rest room he entered and then located the box. He slowly picked up the box placing his hand on the top of it, the box opened.

David removed the eye of Cavoc, placing it around his neck, he then lay on his bed and closed his eyes before falling into a deep sleep. In his dream he entered the fifth dimension.

Cavoc appeared in front of David his face was full of anger. "David come closer and explain how the gold was stolen".

David took a deep breath and stepped forward.

"Look David I can read your mind, it was not your fault Mabus stole the gold he will use it to corrupt and orchestrate his evil".

"Cavoc it was you who recruited him".

"Yes that is correct, his job was to protect you when you arrived in France, he served his purpose did he not? You were born on an island a place of pure evil, if you were ever to return I believe certain death awaits you. Mabus has greed and ambition his master Dogon will be reborn in the nineteenth century the gold is but a war chest. Dogon bring war across all continents and murders millions of Jews vengeance will be his. Mabus betrayed me and if he ever steps foot on French soil again my beasts will rip him to pieces. Our friend Nostradamus was correct when he described Mabus as the Antichrist".

"Cavoc how much longer shall we produce gold?"

"I see it in your eyes you tired of gold after all Bella is your new treasure".

David nodded in agreement.

"Transform the rest of the lead and you will have completed the task at hand. The book and any evidence of transformation must be destroyed".

David agreed and Cavoc began to fade from his dream. David suddenly opened his eyes with a feeling of relief, he removed the eye of Cavoc carefully placing it into the box he then hid the box in a safe place. David smiled to himself as he left the room.

He approached Duval and James, "Good news my friends I have been in contact with Cavoc, our work here is coming to an end, transform the remaining lead and we are finished".

A feeling of warmth and happiness radiated around the old warehouse Duval shook David's hand.

"That is great news my friend soon we will all be very rich," James laughed out loud.

"I shall travel around the world and get fat".

They all laughed together.

"My friends I must leave now and give Bella the good news".

Duval laughed, "It must be love, love, love…"

David smiled then left the warehouse; he started to run as the heavens opened. Rain was something he disliked; he rushed to the guesthouse and knocked on the door. Bella was awaiting his return and opened the door immediately

"Come in quickly such horrible weather I hate the rain".

"Me also my love. Bella let us both be seated I have some good news".

Bella smiled as they both sat down she was glowing in anticipation.

"Bella remember we talked about leaving all of this behind us and moving to Paris? My work here will soon be finished, maybe a couple of weeks or so".

Bella breathed a sigh of relief; she drew closer and kissed David on the lips. He stroked her golden hair; she was full of passion and they continued to kiss.

Bella then laughed, "Well my prince charming when are you going to make an honest woman of me?"

"My princess in a couple of weeks time, you will be all mine".

David embraced Bella, "I must go and help increase production, the time will soon fly".

They kissed once more and then David returned to the warehouse. The rain had now stopped, he could see a rainbow in the distance and he was mesmerised by the colours. All of a sudden Mason appeared.

"Hello David, thank god the rain has stopped. I have exchanged some of the gold for property in Paris and various other Cities in Europe I have lots of papers I need you to sign".

"Good let us go inside and I will sign them".

David knocked on the door after a brief delay Duval opened the door.

"Hello my friends come in and make yourselves at home."

David smiled and spoke, "This way Mason let us discuss business!"

David and Mason walked to the far side of the warehouse the atmosphere was cold with a disagreeable damp smell Mason stopped for a brief second, he rubbed his nose he then began to sneeze.

"Bless you my friend".

Mason wiped his nose then continued to follow David. They both entered the office, the room was full of old cobwebs, in every corner were book shelves, full of old books. David sat down at an old table and invited Mason to join him. Mason placed a case on the table; he reached inside and produced some paper work.

"Right David I need you to sign each of these"

"Oh I heard about Mabus, you always get one rotten apple if you know what I mean?"

David shook his head he was fed up with the name Mabus. David signed the papers.

"Right to business Mason we have over five hundred gold bars can you find a buyer?"

"Yes I have several buyers, I need lots of silver coins for my friends Duval and James have worked so hard".

"Do not worry, they shall have their coins I have spoken to Cavoc, production will soon cease".

"Might I be so bold as to ask what will become of the book?"

"I have been instructed by Cavoc to destroy it".

Mason shook his head in disbelief, "That my friend is such a shame". Mason reached inside his case. "Here I have a present for the lady in your life". He handed David a silver box, David opened it; inside was a collection of jewellery, rings and necklace's David's eyes lit up as he gazed at the precious stones in the box, their quality is truly amazing.

"Right David my business here is now concluded. I will carry on investing the gold into property, do I have your permission to invest in other treasures such as paintings?"

"Yes Mason I have total faith in your investments".

"Thanks David, now I will shake your hand and be about my business".

Mason departed and they shook hands. David closed the box he had a brief conversation with Duval and James then made his way back to Bella. He left the warehouse smiling to himself in contemplation. The silver jewellery box was tucked under his arm. He gazed up to the sky odd rolling white clouds and a rising crimson sun, such a hypnotizing display. David then looked to see Bella standing in the doorway complete with a gleaming smile and a face of cool ivory. David approached Bella complete with a sense of comforting fulfilment.

"Hello Bella let us go inside I have a present for you".

He announced triumphantly Bella laughed and said, "If it is a ring for my finger then you are most welcome".

They both entered the guesthouse. Bella then turned to David, "Come on the suspense is killing me. What is in the box you hold onto so tightly?'

David smiled and handed Bella the silver box, she placed it onto table. As she opened it her eyes sparkled at the sight of the precious jewellery.

"Oh David they are so beautiful, I shall pick out a ring that fits"

Bella tried on several rings until she found the correct size. The ring was silver with in the centre a green emerald. David then announced his undying love for Bella as he knelt down onto one knee and asked, "Will you marry me my love?"

Bella suddenly kissed David passionately and then replied, "Yes I will marry you".

Her eyes sparkled with joy they embraced and kissed.

"We shall be wed in Paris as soon as the work is finished".

Bella took a deep breath and slowly spoke, "The faster you produce the gold the sooner you will be all mine, I wont you to stay in the warehouse to motivate your men to work hard and you will soon be all mine. I have Donna s funeral to attend to, I will go whilst you speed up production so we can escape to Paris".

David smiled and agreed and then returned back to the warehouse, the three friends worked hard together the time flew by. Very soon all the gold was transmuted, a sense of relief filled their hearts with joy. David and Duval gazed at the fruits of their labour; gold as far as the eye could see.

Duval laughed out loud, "my friend, do my eyes deceive me have we really finished all the gold production".

All of a sudden a knock on the door, James opens it and a most welcome face appears, its Mason. He enters the warehouses with two large heavy bags that he drops on the cold floor. The noise echoes all around the old warehouse. Mason looks to Duval and James, "A bag for each of you, silver coins, this is but a small percentage owed to you my friends. I will return with another bag tomorrow and so on until you have your correct payment. You my friends shall live like kings".

Duval starts to dance towards the bag of silver; James picks up a bag and places it on the table. He opens it slowly a broad grin, a shake of the head and he places his hands amongst the silver coins mesmerised. He bursts out into laughter, "Oh how I love the sight of silver, the world is my oyster. I shall travel around the world, cross the seven seas. The first thing I will need is a couple of servants to carry my silver".

Duval laughs, "It seems like a very good idea my friend. I shall do the same a couple of pretty servant girls will do me fine. A roar of laughter echoed all around the old warehouse Mason approached David.

"I cannot leave you out, here". Mason handed David a pouch full of silver coins, "This is just the beginning you will be well looked after".

Mason reached into his pocket and then produced some papers, "I have purchased a Mansion in the Latin Quarter, a district dominated by universities, colleges and prestigious high schools. It is situated on the left bank of the Seine, Paris is circular, the people describe it as an egg. The wealthy west and the poor east. Paris my friend is also full of hazards. I have witnessed the poor eat dead dogs from the gutters. There are rumours and legends of Satan's presence in Paris, it is a Catholic stronghold. Protestants end up with their throats cut whilst they are in Paris, never mention your religious beliefs or lack of them. I have sent word to all the local merchants they will deliver your food and drink. You will wont for nothing. I have also appointed a housekeeper her name is Shana, she is very honest and reliable".

David smiles, "Thank you Mason, where would we all be without you?"

"I serve you as I do Cavoc, he has spoke to me in my dreams, he wants me to invest and protect the gold. Thus I have employed twenty-five guards to protect the gold. All are trusted men that have sworn allegiance to the cause, never worry the gold will be is quite safe".

David shook Masons hand, "Oh one more thing David, I have arranged for a carriage to pick you and Bella up tomorrow morning. Be prepared for the long journey to Paris, you leave the rest to me".

David shared the news with his friends they embraced and said farewell.

Mason grinned, "Go now David, inform the beautiful Bella of the good news".

David left immediately surrounded by a comforting sense of relief and fulfilment, he walked over to the guesthouse and he slowly knocked on the door. Bella opened the door and David was greeted by a face of true beauty. A warm smile; he took a deep breath then spoke of the carriage picking them up in the morning, "Finally my love, we will be in Paris where a large Mansion awaits. We shall want for nothing".

Bella s eyes light up, "oh David this is like a dream come true, come closer let us embrace".

David closed the door, they then embraced and kissed.

Bella smiled then spoke softly, "My prince, I shall have to pack all of my belongings".

David turned to the table and slowly emptied the contents of his pouch onto the table, the sound of falling silver coins echoed all around the room.

"I shall replace all of your belongings, you shall have the finest clothes in Paris, you will want for nothing".

Bella laughed and said, "I cannot wait, a fresh new start in Paris. What more could a princess want".

Bella took hold of David's hand, kissing him on the cheek, "David are you hungry or thirsty?"

"No, sleep that's what I need."

Bella agreed and took him to the bedroom, they kissed for a while and very soon David's eyes began to close. He lay down and fell into a deep sleep. It was soon morning, the sun shone through the window. David opened his eyes he blinked and then he heard the noise banging on the front door.

He climbed out of bed and dashed down the stairs opening the front door with great haste. There stood at the doorway was a tall man dressed in black, a craggy face and long pointed nose.

"Hello sir, I have your carriage ready. I am to take you to Paris".

David took a deep breath, "Thank you give me five minutes to get ready".

"Yes sir, take as long as you like. I have been well paid".

David hurried back up the stairs into the bedroom. Bella had overheard the conversation and was getting dressed for the long journey to Paris. Bella had a small trunk with her few belongings packed inside. David reached for his trunk containing the eye of Cavoc and the book of transformation. It was such a treasure he could not destroy it. David looked to Bella, a sigh of relief as he gazed into her ice blue eyes and said, "Are you ready? Our destiny awaits".

Bella smiled, David picked up the luggage and they then proceeded to the awaiting carriage. The driver stood motionless, suddenly he spoke with in a deep gravely voice, "Let me take the luggage sir".

The door was open, David looked to Bella, "Ladies first".

Bella laughed as she climbed inside the carriage. David followed, closing the door behind him. The driver climbed up to his seat, a crack of a whip and they where on the way to Paris. Bella shaded her eyes from the bright dazzling morning sun. David sank into his seat closing his eyes for a brief second. Bella looked at David steadily in the face smiling to herself in contentment.

David closed his eyelids once more, memories of the past year flashing before him. So much had happened and then a soft reassuring voice told David everything was alright, you look so tied. David slowly opened his eyes wide and spoke quietly.

"So much has happened to me in the past year, good and bad. I often wish I could predict the future".

"Look David do not worry, we have each other. Close your eyes again, let your mind be at peace".

David once more closed his eyes, the journey was long and tiresome and very soon Bella also fell asleep. David was awoken by Bella, "David we have arrived in Paris".

He opened his eyes and took a deep breath; he then leaned forward and embraced Bella. "Finally we have reached our destination". The carriage door opened slowly the driver stood before them a clear face of relief his work was done.

"Good evening sir and madam," the driver spoke ever so politely. "I have your luggage, follow me and I will escort you to your new dwelling". Bella took hold of David's hand and stepped out of the carriage it had been raining Bella began to walk stepping into a puddle, she laughed then began to shake her head. The sky was grey, the sound of the howling wind echoed all around as they followed the driver to a large mansion. It was a magnificent building, all of a sudden a small pretty girl appeared from within, "Hello sir and madam, my name is Shana. I am your housekeeper".

Shana was petite, complete with a warm and friendly smile. David and Bella introduced themselves. Shana spoke to the driver who then moved sharply into the mansion placing the luggage onto a table. Shana looked to the sky, quickly David and Bella rushed inside as a thunderstorm broke out over the city. David gazed all around, the mansion was fully furnished. He then turned his attention to the focal point of the room, the large fireplace. The flames left David mesmerised for a brief second.

Bella smiled then spoke, "David the mansion is beautiful is it not?"

The architecture was so pleasing to the eye, typical of the renaissance period. The driver smiled then said goodbye, disappearing into the storm.

David looked to Shana, "You knew the storm was about to strike didn't you?"

"Yes master, I have a sense for these things. I believe I inherited the sight from my poor departed mother, her name was Helen she was such a beautiful lady. She died of the plague along with my father and brother".

Bella walked over to Shana and embraced her, "I lost my parents to the plague also. Such a waste of lives".

Shana put on a brave face, "I have prepared a little nightcap". She pointed to the table where two drinking vessels and a vintage bottle of wine were. Shana poured out the red wine and David and Bella quenched their thirsts.

Right let me show you around, first the kitchen and then the large study, complete with bookshelves. They then made their way upstairs to the bedrooms, the wind howled as it rained without easing. Shana smiled as they reached the end of the long corridor, "Here we are the master bedroom".

Shana opened the door; she said goodnight then disappeared into the shadows. They entered the bedroom

Bella's eyes lit up at the sight of the king-size four-posted bed. She smiled and said, "This room is fit for a queen">

Bella slowly turned towards David, passionately kissing him on the lips. They continued to kiss and made love until the early hours. The following day Shana took David and Bella on a tour of the rest of the mansion. David found the fully-stocked library very appealing. He sat for hours reading books whilst Shana and Bella purchased new clothes, one item in particular made her smile with delight; a wedding dress. They soon got married and live life to the full, several months later Bella announced she was pregnant.

She gave birth to a healthy baby boy they called him David, his parents wanted the best for him and he was educated at the finest schools. His father told him about Nostradamus and the fifth dimension on his fifteenth birthday. David was taken into the study and shown a book his father had just completed, it was entitled *The Five Fives.* He sat listening to his fathers words of wisdom, "There is no greater power than the written word, a book will live on until the end of time. My son I have something else to show you". He reached inside a draw and then produced a strange object.

"What is it father?"

"This is to be handed on throughout history, our bloodline is the key".

He placed the strange looking object onto the table.

"Father it looks a small Egyptian pyramid, may I take a closer look?"

"Yes son, I want you to open it".

David placed his hands on top of the pyramid, it opened up. Inside David gazed motionless, mesmerised at the sight of the eye of Cavoc.

"Father this is the eye of Cavoc and these the cards".

"Yes son that is correct, the man that visits us. Mason. He is the keeper of the gold. Yes he has served Cavoc well purchasing property all over Europe and the new world. He is our greatest asset, once I have departed from this world you must continue with my work. One day you will have a son and you will teach him what I have taught you".

"Father, you spoke of a man by the name of Nostradamus? I have heard my friends talk of this man they say he is a remarkable physician, mathematician and astrologer".

"Your friends are correct," he is all of these things and much more. "Cavoc told me Nostradamus will publish the first edition of his book *Centuries* in the year fifteen fifty-five. The book will contain predictions of future events, Nostradamus is a good man, he helped me cross over to the fifth dimension. In the twentieth century millions will talk of him being the greatest seer of all time.

"You know so much father".

"Yes Cavoc has taught me wisely".

"Father, my friend Peter went to listen to a lecture on astrology, mathematics and alchemy. The man is from England, his name is John Dee".

Bella suddenly appeared.

"David a stranger called John is at the front door, he says he seeks your divine attention".

David looked to his son in a state of shock and confusion. David made his way to the front door, in them doorway stood a tall slender handsome man with a mystical appearance.

"Do not be frightened David my name is John Dee. I only seek conversation; I was told you have a vast collection of books. You know so much about me, yes the angel Uriel told me all about you. I am in Paris doing lectures".

"This is so strange, my son informed me about your lectures five minutes later you stand before me. Numbers my friend are the basis of all things and the key to knowledge".

John then stepped forward and held out his hand in friendship, they shook hands and embraced.

"Right my friend without further a do, show me to your library. I hunger for enlightenment".

David smiled and then guided John to the library, once inside John was amazed at the collection of books from all around Europe and the middle-east. John was like a child in a candy shop, he was one of the most learned men of his age.

"A book on summoning and one on Hermetic magic; may I borrow these books please David".

John picked out the books as David nodded his head.

"Now David let us be seated and engage in intellectual conversation".

"Here John let us sit down here".

They both sat around a small round oak table, "David me and you have a lot in common, we both talk to Angels and have scientific and occult interests. I am a crystal gazer I know all about the book of transmutation Cavoc stole from Cabal the Jew. You produced tonnes of gold, something I can only dream of. The angel Uriel asked me to visit you with a warning beware of the fifth child of Henry. One day you will have a burning desire to return to England".

"You must never return; the Anti-Christ Mabus would hunt you down like a dog, he still craves your gold".

"My friend I will never return to England. Paris is my home".

"Good, may I ask you about Cavoc? You first visited him with the aid of Nostradamus. You are truly blessed. You know so much John".

"Yes the angels keep me well informed on the universal language of creation, a balance of good and evil The five fives. Uriel has also warned me in five years on the fifth month I am to be arrested, charged with being a conjurer. A Star Chamber prosecution. He told me not to worry as he has plans for me in the sixteenth century. The Golden Age; he has spoken of it on several occasions. Elizabeth will be Queen and shall play a role in her politics. Now my friend I must go, it has been a pleasure meeting you".

John picked up the books, "I still have so much to learn".

David looked up into John's hypnotic eyes, "Yes take the books with my blessing".

John picked up the books he grinned broadly then spoke in a strange language, his words radiated a deep sense of peace, 'My that was a prayer for the living, I hope one day our paths cross again".

"Goodbye David," John left as he arrived in a shroud of mystery.

Bella suddenly appeared asking, "David who was that strange man? His name is John Dee, a scholar seeking knowledge; one extraordinary man".

Bella laughed then walked over to David and kissed him on the cheek, "My husband, we have everything we need we want for nothing, will we always be so lucky?"

David gazed into Bella's eyes and drew a deep breath always my wife, always.

He then embraced Bella; the years flew by and then a visit from an old friend. Duval, his face had changed, riddled with battle scars, he had fought in various wars for his king and country. The two friends embraced and sat drinking wine and exchanging stories next to a raging open fire. The sounds of laughter echoed all around the room.

David looked to Duval, "My friend, will you stay here with us for a while we have plenty of room?"

Shana entered the room with more wine.

Duval smiled, "thank you my pretty one".

She placed the open bottle of wine on the table then left smiling. David laughed then spoke out again, "Duval you haven't answered my question".

"Thank you for your gracious invitation, but I must decline".

David looked at Duval in confusion. Duval smiled from ear to ear then burst out laughing, "I jest my friend".

He had not lost his strange sense of humour, the wine was strong very soon they where both falling asleep. Bella appeared shaking her head, "Come on David let us escort your friend to the spare bedroom".

Duval rubbed his eyes, "Am I in heaven? Stood before me I see an angel".

All three laughed out loud, Duval was shown to the bedroom where he fell straight to sleep. Bella smiled at David as she helped him into their bed, "My dear husband it has been a while since I heard such laughter. Duval was and always will be your best friend".

David nodded his head then fell into a deep sleep. The following day a messenger arrived from England, he handed David a sealed letter from his sister. Bella and Duval looked on as David opened the letter

He began to read it slowly, his heart was beating faster and faster at the news he had always dreaded. Bella drew closer, her eyes filled with terror.

"David what does the letter say?" With a sad and dazed look David spoke. "The letter is from my sister Carol, her husband has been robbed and killed. She was beaten to within an inch of her life, she now lies bedridden".

Memories of his sister's kindness came flooding back to David, he then put on a brave face as he then spoke slowly.

"Before I left my sister I promised I would return and visit her once more, it is something I must do".

Bella started to panic and then gave a wild cry of horror, "No I do not want to loose you, returning to England would be suicide remember Mabus, what he said? Pure evil awaits you if you return to England".

A sense of doom engulfed the room, Duval looked to David, "If you go to England I shall go with you and protect you".

Tears trickled down Bella's cheeks; she shook her head in disbelief. David had a vision of his sister calling out his name from her deathbed.

"I am truly sorry Bella. My mind is made up I have hidden away from Mabus for too long, he is but one man".

Duval looked to David and spoke, I have a friend a merchant who could get us across the channel under the cover of darkness, we could be there and back in twenty-four hours".

Bella knew David had made his mind up, nothing she could do or say would change his mind, she wiped away her tears and then clenched David's hand, "Tell me what I must do if you do not return".

David collected his thoughts and with fixed eyes he stared towards Duval. "The merchant you speak of, are you sure we can trust him with our lives?

"Yes, I have known him for many years, he has a small boat. I know where he is staying it isn't far from here in fact. I had a drink with him last week, his daughter is so beautiful".

Bella gazed at Duval, "Do you promise to bring back my husband?"

Duval stood tall with a stern fixed expression he said, "Yes,' he then reached for his sword. "For many years I have fought for worthy causes, with this sword I have killed many. I consider this to be ultimate cause. Do not worry I shall not fail your husband".

Bella forced a smile; she then closed her eyes whilst entrancing her husband. A brief silence and then David spoke, "Bella if by some chance I do not return I want you to carry on doing what you do best, looking after what is precious to me; our son and our investments such as these four walls".

Bella smiled, "Do not worry David I will carry on looking after what is precious to you".

"Bella if anything should happen to me and Duval send word to Mason and James". David kissed Bella tenderly he then drew a deep breath, all of a sudden his son appeared he looked to his father sensing something wasn't right with a blink and a frown he then spoke, "I overheard the conversation you are to return to England. Can I come with you? I have learnt to fight with a sword"

"No my brave son you must stay here and look after your mother. One day Cavoc will visit you as he did with me, we must not fail him, the bloodline must continue. We have had many conversations on this matter you know what you must do my son".

David's heart was filled with sorrow and he had a bad feeling he wouldn't be coming back, "Come here son".

David walked over to his father and embraced him, with a look of concern. "But father you haven't got a weapon, here take my dagger".

"Look son, I have no need of a weapon".

"Please father take it with you".

"Oh alright then".

David attached the dagger to his belt and he smiled, "Come on let us all embrace".

They all embraced each other".

"I must go now, Duval let us go to the stables. I will see both of you very soon, remember take care of business whilst I am gone' now goodbye". David turned and accompanied Duval to the stables, once there they mounted their horses then galloped to the Merchants' House.

David followed Duval, the sunlight was bright David glanced up at the birds on the wing. The summer breeze whistled all around, very soon they arrived at their destination. The merchant was standing outside his house he looked up at a familiar face. Duval slowed his horse and then with lightning speed dismounted from his horse, he then spoke to the merchant.

"Judas my friend, I have a favour to ask of you I want you to take me and my friend David on your boat across the Channel to England".

"Well Duval, this evening I don't know I have things to do".

"I will make it worth your while, here are five silver coins. Two now, three when we return. We intend on staying for only a few hours, a quick visit".

"Duval my friend, you know I cannot say no to silver coins".

David looked at Judas, his dark sinister eyes, a weather beaten face and heavy dark eyebrows. Duval handed Judas the silver coins and he licked his lips with a sinister expression on his face.

"Thank you Duval, now wait here whilst I get my horse."

David dismounted from his horse he then confronted Duval with a sense of doom. "My friend you did not mention the fact his name was Judas, there is something sinister about him. Are you sure we can trust him?"

Duval laughed out loud, "Yes of course, this is the reaction I expected. That is why I never mentioned his name".

David shook his head and took a deep breath, "Perhaps Duval I am being paranoid. I just remember it was Judas who betrayed Jesus in the Bible".

All of a sudden Judas appeared, "Is everything alright Duval?"

"Yes let us go to the boat they mounted their horses and rode with great haste to the boat. Two days later they arrived at the boat and were soon sailing across the channel to England. Judas had a small crew on board, the light faded rapidly and the cry of the wind echoed all around the small boat docked under the cover of darkness.

"Right Judas stay here and wait for us, when we all set sail at sunrise you shall have the rest of your silver">

Judas grinned and then shouted to his men to help with the horses. Very soon the two horses where on dry land once more the two mounted their horses and began to gallop towards his sisters dwelling.

The stars shone bright, David's mind began to fill with excitement. Once again he would be reunited with his sister, faster and faster they rode, both almost breathless with fatigue and then the sight out of the darkness he had waited to see for so long; his sisters dwelling. A draft of cold air suddenly ran down his spine. David slowed down and then spoke to Duval, this is the place let us proceed with great caution. David could hear the sound of a startled crow, he had fear in his eyes, slowly and solemnly they moved.

A sense of doom engulfed his every move, David and Duval dismounted from their horses, they could see a light in the bedroom and in the hallway. Duval looked into David's eyes, he could sense his fear.

"My friend, do you want me to wait here with the horses whilst you visit your sister?"

"No Duval we have crossed many miles you must be parched come inside and have a drink".

"Thank you my friend"

David knocked on the door and after a brief delay the door opened. In the doorway stood an old lady, her eyes wide open.

"Who might you be in this ungodly hour?"

"I am David, Carols brother".

"Oh good, come in I have heard so much about you. My name is Helen I have been looking after your poor sister, she is in a bad way. Her husband Edwin was robbed, his throat cut from ear to ear. These are dark times we live in">

The old woman was short with a strange completion and accent. She escorted David to his sister, whilst Duval quenched his thirst.

Helen opened the bedroom door and smiled, "Right David, I expect you want to be all alone with your sister. I will fix your friend some supper".

David nodded; he then put on a brave face and entered the room. He looked to the bed, his sister sat up her face pale and pain and anxiety twisted her face. Her left eye was swollen shut, frowning in confusion she spoke with wild terror in her eyes.

"Who's that, who's there?"

Without hesitation David spoke, "My sister, it is me David".

"Tears began to trickle from her eyes, "Oh my brother, David you promised one day you would return to see me. I just wish under happier circumstances".

David remembered his sister before he left for France, she was such a beauty. His sorrow turned to anger, "Who did this to you?"

Carol took a deep breath and then spoke, "Six men dressed in black, their faces covered attacked me and Edwin. I remember their leader he had such evil eyes, he killed Edwin then repeatedly beat me until I told him where we kept our silver. They took all we had, thirty pieces of silver".

David embraced his sister, tears came to his eyes. His heart was full of sorrow and he sensed somehow he was to blame for his sister's pain and suffering. David felt the heat; his sister was burning with fever. Her frail hands began to shake. Helen then entered the room with a jug of water.

"David she needs rest, I will nurse her. You join your friend and get some sleep, you can talk some more in the morning".

David kissed his sister on the cheek, "Until tomorrow then".

Carol forced a smile but her body cried out in pain. David then left Helen with his sister rejoining his friend Duval.

He sat next to him rubbing his tearful eyes. Duval finished off his drink then spoke, "David you look shattered. How bad is your sister?"

"Duval she is battered and bruised and burning with fever, her face is as pale as death. I fear she will not recover. My mind is full of thoughts of the evil that has gone on here, my sister said the men that robbed and murdered her husband where dressed in black. Their leader possessed such eyes of evil, maybe it was Mabus?"

"David no. Forget about Mabus, we need our sleep we will return to France tomorrow like we planned".

David was completely exhausted his eyes closed and he then fell into a deep sleep. In the land of dreams his whole world flashed before him, he remembered John Dee and the words he spoke, "If you return to England Mabus would hunt you down like a dog". Both of his parents appeared in his dream, they both suffered tragic endings and now his sister. All of a sudden an old woman began to shake David.

She cried out, "Wake up, wake up".

"He opened his eyes, it was now morning.

"Your sister, she has passed away, she must have died in her sleep".

Duval woke up listening to the cries of the old woman. David leapt to his feet. He knew he had overslept, in a state of panic he rushed over to his sister's deathbed. He felt for a pulse in a state of disbelief. Nothing. She was stone cold, he sank onto the bed, anger and sorrow filled his troubled soul. Helen began to weep uncontrollably she then remembered the last words his sister spoke in a haunting voice.

"She mentioned the name of the murderer, she said he was the Antichrist. His name was Mabus".

David's face reflected a shade of terror, panic then set in and he shouted, "My god this must be a trap. I must warn my friend".

David raced over to Duval, his eyes filled with wild terror.

"Duval we must leave immediately, all that has happened, it's all the evil work of Mabus".

Duval jumped to his feet in a state of shock, he looked outside in a confused state and then yelled. "Quick to our horse's.

David opened the door; he was then gripped by a hot flush panic. The horses had disappeared. David gazed fearfully all around. Before him in the distance stood men-at-arms. David and Duval where completely surrounded. All of a sudden a tall dark figure appeared it was Mabus. He moved forward his deep loud voice echoed all around as he moved closer and closer. He then stopped. David gazed at his evil grin, his eyes dark as hell. He laughed to himself then spoke,

"Welcome back to England David and of course your friend Duval. Tell me where the gold is located and I will spare your lives".

David looked into the cold dark evil eyes of Mabus and spoke, "You are so evil I shall have my vengeance and send you back to hell where you belong".

Mabus broke out in laughter; his men saw the funny side and also began to laugh. Mabus then composed himself standing tall he spoke with great confidence. "My brave fool that is not going to happen. I have fifty men, you are completely surrounded and you have no boat home your friend Judas betrayed you for the fifty pieces of silver that I stole from your sister".

Duval placed his hands on his head in disbelief he then gritted his teeth in anger he drew his sword.

Mabus smiled with barbaric delight, "Ah Duval you are a fighter. You five test his metal".

Five men-at-arms moved forward with swords drawn. Duval turned to David and spoke with determination and authority, "Stand behind me, this is the way I dreamt I would die".

David shouted to his friend, "No Duval".

A clash of steel. Duval swung his sword cutting down his opponents with great ease, their blood spurted out with every stroke of his blade and he fought with great frenzy. Duval turned a slashing blow and then a thrust of his sword and five men lay dead. Mabus began to clap; he had gained sadistic pleasure from the sword fight.

"You are good Duval, too good. I can't waste any more men, what would the queen think".

Mabus called over five men armed with crossbows. In a dominant voice he shouted, "You men finish him off".

The five raised their crossbows taking aim and then they fired their high velocity bolts, before Duval could react all five hit the target. Duval fell to his knees. David rushed his friend's aid. It was too late, blood poured from his wounds. David then felt a blow to his head; he fell to the ground his eyes closed leaving him in total darkness. A soldier under the orders of Mabus had crept up behind David clubbing across his head. Mabus smiled condescendingly and with an edge of coldness he shouted to his men, "Take him to the Tower".

Later on David awoke in pain, the wound on the top of his head caused him such agony. He was confused, his ankles fastened and his wrists chained. A smell of dampness the light was poor this was hell. Mabus suddenly appeared from the shadows, David reflected a shade of terror as he gazed into his cold dark eyes.

"Dark regards David, pain is what I am all about. Your friend Duval died a hero, you will die a coward. I will have you crying out for mercy. Queen Mary has granted me five days to torture you at will, tell me all about the gold and I will spare your life. You shall suffer no more pain. I grow angry and inpatient if your silence mocks me. Oh well down to business.

"You are on the rack; this is a torture device of which I have many".

Attendants appeared with flickering candles. Mabus looked to David, 'My you look tense. I am going to loosen you up a bit".

An attendant operated a handle increasing the tension on the chains as David was slowly being stretched. The pain was so intense, his wrists started to swell; a gripping pain and then blood began oozing from his wounds. David gritted his teeth. A wailing choking scream echoed all around from another victim of torture. Mabus shook his head, "Right that's enough".

He then turned his attention to David, "Still such silence. I know how far to go; any more tension and your joints would be dislocated and eventually separated. Next a popping noise as your bones snap like twigs. Look around David, on show is every device and instrument of human torture, which one would you like to try out next?"

David took a deep breath, his whole body ached with pain, his mouth was so dry as he then spoke, "Mabus may you rot in hell, either let ether let me go or kill me as I will never betray Cavoc".

"You finally speak but it is not what I wanted to hear from you. I have never failed to gain a confession; I have tortured hundreds of men, woman and children. I must admit I enjoy my job. Where is the gold?'

All of a sudden out of the shadows a hideous sight; it was Quino a seasoned servant of torture. Short, stocky

FIVE FIVES

and ugly. Mabus smiled, "Oh there you are Quino, cut off his big toe and then throw him back into the dungeon. I have other business to attend to. I shall see you later".

Mabus then turned around and walked off into the darkness. Quino looked at David with a grin of cold malice. He started to mumble, "Did my master say left or right? Which toe is it to be, hmm let me see".

This was horror beyond David's worst nightmare. Extreme terror engulfed David's mind, without warning Quino ran a blade up and down David s left foot. He then cut off David's little toe the pain was so great David passed out. Quino stood mumbling to himself, "Master stupid, if I would have cut off his big toe he would not be able to walk and show him the gold">

Quino with the aid of a guard carried David to the coldest, darkest and dampest dungeon. Several hours later David awoke shivering in pain. The door suddenly opened it was Quino. He shouted, "Come on, its feeding time".

He was holding a dish of slops. "Why you looking at me like that David? It aint for you its for my pet rats".

He then threw the dish of slops into the corner of the dungeon where the rats had assembled. "Look at them feast David, they're so hungry. See you tomorrow, sleep tight don't let the rodents bite".

David shook his head; with so much evil on display was there a way out? He closed his eyes the sounds of rats scurrying around echoed in the dungeon, he dreamt he was being eaten, the pain of something chewing on his flesh. He opened his eyes in extreme horror, the rats where eating away at his feet and ankles. He cried out at the top of his voice, the door opened it was Mabus. In his hand a flaming torch he waved it chasing the rats away. Once more David passed out. Mabus stood, his anger reached boiling point and he shouted for the guards. Two guards entered the dungeon, "get him out of here now. If he dies there will be no gold, take him upstairs and clean up his wounds. Where is Quino? I will make him suffer".

All of a sudden Quino appeared, "What is it master?"

Mabus picked him up off the ground, he possessed supernatural strength and he then threw Quino against the dungeon wall, "I left you in charge whilst I carried out a few murders for our Queen Mary. I return to this? Did I give you permission to feed him to the rats?"

A stunned injured Quino looked up to his master, "I am so sorry master".

"If he dies before I say so, you will join him. Do I make myself clear?"

"Yes master it wont happen again".

"It better not".

Mabus then left Quino to pick himself up off the cold floor. David woke up one hour later, he was in a bed, his wounds had been treated and he was dressed in clean clothes. Before he could climb out of bed Mabus appeared, "Good you are awake, you tend to sleep a lot don't you? Anyway I have prepared a banquet, come on hurry out of bed this way. The last thing I want to do is starve you to death".

David followed Mabus to the next room; a large table had been set out full of various foods. David was starving and he rushed over to the food and began to feast and drink. Mabus watched with his burning eyes and cruel smile. "My David you love that red wine, it numbs the pain does it not?"

David sat back on the chair; he knew this was his last meal. Mabus then sat down and spoke, "Right David let us talk for a while. Remember back to when I took the gold, the men that assisted me moving the gold to England. Oh how I trusted them, once in England we celebrated in a tavern, we drank and drank for several hours. For the first time I made the mistake of letting my guard down. I sat half asleep and one of the men crept up behind me, he clubbed me to the back of the head several times. They thought they had left me for dead. I do not die easily. I soon tracked them down along with my gold. I made them pay for their treachery.

"The head injury I sustained left me with no memory of transformation. The book, what became of the Jews book did you destroy it David?

Without hesitation he confirmed the book had been destroyed, a simple nod of the head was sufficient. Mabus shook him in disgust. "Such a shame, imagine the value of such a book. Truly priceless. David took another sip of wine and then looked to Mabus and spoke.

"Why did Cavoc ever trust one so evil as you?"

"I believe it was fate, mine and your destiny. Cavoc enlisted me because he knew I was the only person that could get you to Montpellier safely. The roads were full of bandits, if I had not been in the carriage the thieves would have slit your throat. Did I ever tell you about Nostradamus he feared me, he knew I was evil. I asked him for help he refused calling me the Antichrist. John Dee taught me how to crystal gaze. I saw my master Dogon; he is to be reborn in Austria in the year nineteen hundred and four. He will seize control of Hitler and inhabit his body, later he will talk of returning Germany to glory. His hypnotic eyes will have total mind control over the German people. They will become zombies, servants of my master. The Christian church will know of the demonic possession. By this time he will be too powerful. World domination, destruction, mass genocide. Dogon will remember how he was slain in his past life, poisoned by the Jews. He will extract his revenge and go all out to exterminate them off the face of the planet. He will then conquer the whole world".

David smiled then began to laugh, "I have heard this story before, but with a completely different outcome".

Mabus snarled, "How dare you mock, the crystal never lies. John Dee has shown me. Never mind I will have the last laugh watching you suffer and die. My

Queen, or should I say Bloody Mary is bitter and obsessive. I mentioned to her about her hellfire policy, now she believes it is essential to cleanse the land of the work of the Devil".

David looked to Mabus, "But the greatest Devil sits across the table from me, you are the Antichrist".

"Well David, yes I suppose your right. This is to be a busy year for me. Queen Mary has handed me a list of Protestants she wants tortured and killed. I know you have lived in Paris like a king for many years; a man visited you by the name of John Dee. I have spoken to him on this matter. Did you know he reads horoscopes for the Queen? He is a seeker of knowledge, a mystic at heart. A real enthusiast of the occult, he believes the number five is the key to the secrets of the universe. The five fives. Your friend Cavoc is but a distant memory, anyway back to John.

I have informed my Queen about his calculating he has cast horoscopes of Queen Mary and Princess Elizabeth. I believe the charges will expand to treason against Mary after you have departed from this realm. John Dee will take your place; my men seek more evidence as we speak. David, back to our little problem, tell me about the gold or I shall inflict more pain onto you".

David gazed onto the table a bread knife came into view Mabus laughs, "Oh David, pick it up. I have no weapon. I imagine this will be your last chance to escape".

David reached for the knife. Mabus stood up and laughed. Demonic laughter echoed all around the room. "David have you got a tight grip of the knife? It is made of solid silver that knife could kill me. This is the only chance you will get to put an end to my evil, give it your best shot".

David tightly gripped the knife his anger override his fear. He shouted, "You killed my sister".

"Yes so I did. I also killed your best friend Duval. Such anger, I feel your anger".

David lunged forward reddened with rage his heart was pounding and he fought with great frenzy inflicting a wound on Mabus. Blood spurted out of his arm, a sadistic scream and then an almighty blow to David's head sent him flying across the table. The supernatural blow had knocked David clean out, Mabus snarled, "guards".

Three guards entered the room. He shouted, "Take him back to the dungeon".

Quino appeared, "Master your arm".

"Yes, it is but a scratch. Have him ready for more interrogation in two hours, do I make myself clear".

"Yes master".

David was returned to the dungeon, he dreamt of angels. A bright light and then a softly spoken voice rang out in his mind. "David you have been so brave your ordeal is far from over, you have shown true devotion. I just wish there was some way I could help you".

All of a sudden David was awoken by a bucket of ice cold water thrown over him by Quino. David shivered through his frame and he gritted his teeth and then shouted in vain. David began to cough he was escorted back to the torture chamber he was then chained hanging by his wrists from an oak beam. Mabus stood before him he began to laugh out loud, "What have I told you about sleeping all the time".

David looked at Mabus he had nothing to lose. He knew his fate was death.

Mabus smiled, "Oh my arm. Do not fear, it is but a scratch. An eye for an eye that is what I say. Quino it is time; the whip".

Quino ripped open the back of David's shirt he then stood back as the whip came down on his back. His skin ripped apart, blood splattered everywhere. David cried out in pain.

Mabus grinned, "Right Quino I must go. I have an audience with the Queen I wont be long. The year is fifteen fifty-five let him have fifty-five lashes. Remember Quino count if you must".

"Yes master, stop for a minute and count to fifty, then proceed. Practice makes perfect. I have learnt to count to fifty".

"Well let me hear you".

Quino began to count to fifty; Mabus shook his head and left. Quino carried on counting after twenty he became confused. "Now what's after twenty/"

David began to laugh which made Quino angry; he cracked the whip against David's back. Once more he cried out in pain. Wailing, choking sounds echoed all around. David closed his eyes, the white light returned once more, as did the angel. She smiled and spoke in a warm soft voice "Let us talk, I am here to help. I cannot watch you suffer any more. T he best I can do is to banish your pain. Look into my eyes".

The angel radiated a deep sense of warmth; another crack of the whip David became excited. "The pain, I feel no pain".

The angel smiled, "Good, Cavoc will be proud of me, now I must go".

The angel disappeared as Mabus returned. David opened his eyes as Quino continued to crack the whip. Mabus gazed into David's eyes in confusion. "You feel no pain? You feel no pain. Quino stop now".

Mabus stood wild eyed, thinking what could have happened. He spoke of his fears, "I know what happened, an angel visited you when I was gone didn't she?'

David laughed for the first time in ages, "Yes she was so beautiful I now feel no pain".

"I waste my time Quino. I need time to think, take him back to the dungeon; there is more than one way to skin a cat.

David was returned to the dungeon he sat in the corner mesmerised by a glimmer of light, he then closed his eyes and fell into a deep sleep. The following day he awoke and he took a deep breath. Memories of his wife and son came flooding back to him. The door of the dungeon suddenly opened it was Mabus in his hand a piece of paper, "Look David you have failed me so the Queen has signed your death warrant. I told her under torture you had admitted to sorcery, the date of your execution well it had to be the fifth of the fifth fifteen fifty-five. What a treat five fives is it not?"

David looked at Mabus, a glaring face and death cold eyes he then spoke with confidence, "Cavoc shall reap vengeance on you".

Mabus laughed, "oh is that so? Do I look frightened? He lacks the power to cross over to my domain".

David shook his head and spoke, "Your domain?"

"Yes my domain. I have the power over life and death. Yours. You shall be burnt at the stake as did Joan of Arc. What you show no emotion, it doesn't bother you? I forgot you don't feel pain do you? But your family. Oh but the light of foresight I questioned John Dee. He told me all about your library, the location of your family. I now see anger in your eyes he is the innocent party; I told him I was an old friend. He doesn't even know you are here, after your death I will take a party of my finest men cross the channel and kill your family and collect the gold".

David shook with wild terror he then shouted, "No you cannot destroy the bloodline".

"What. I do as I please, who can stop me? It is but your own doing. You wouldn't speak, but I am sure your family will be very accommodating".

David got to his feet pulling on his chains that held him down. Mabus grinned, "Let us say no more on this subject. I have things to prepare. I will see you tomorrow at your burning; I must admit I wouldn't miss it for the world. I am afraid it wont fetch much of a crowd, as no one knows you".

Mabus then turned laughing as he left David clenched his frail hands. He drew a deep breath and shouted, "You cannot destroy my bloodline. Cavoc help me, help my family".

He then fell to his feet a cold perspiration spread all over his body as he fell into a deep sleep. The next day David lay on the cold floor, his body shivered but still no pain. He then had flash backs of his father and the tales he once told the maid of Orleans. It seemed he was going to share the same fate, burnt at the stake.

Five knocks on the dungeon door and then Mabus entered complete with his usual sinister smile and cold evil eyes. "Right guards, take him to the stake. It's time for David burns to burn".

The guards lifted David from the floor removing his chains, he was then escorted out of the dungeon up a set of draughty cold stone stairs and then down a dark tunnel. At the end of the tunnel light. David was taken outside the light hurt his eyes, such sunshine. David shielded his eyes, he then regained his composure more and more guards appeared.

Mabus shouted to his men, "Hurry up tie him to the stake. I have business to attend to in Paris".

David began to struggle as several guards manhandled and tied him to the stake. A crowd started to gather, a Bishop read out David last rites, "Is there anything you require my son?"

David remembered. The story of the Maid of Orleans he then asked for a Cross. The Bishop shook his head and spoke, "I am sorry Mabus has given me strict instructions he forbids you from having a Cross as you are a heretic?"

"Why do you take orders from Mabus, he is but the Antichrist. I myself have the faith of the five fives".

The Bishop looked at David's wounds in confusion and spoke, "Why you feel no pain nor fear death?"

David smiled, "I feel no pain as I have a guardian angel looking after me".

"What?"

"I know all of this is beyond your comprehension">

"No my son you speak blasphemous language. Are you sure it is the work of an angel?"

David smiled as the Bishop swiftly moved away. Mabus then shouted, "Right men pile up the faggots".

A cold shiver ran down David's spine, the crowd got bigger and bigger as David looked up at the burning sun and then to the crowd who were puzzled by David's defiant attitude. The fire was lit, David gazed into the fire mesmerised by the flames but he had no fear as he felt no pain. A flaring light of flames rose higher and higher, it was not the ending he had dreamt of. He felt all alone as he looked up and shouted to the heavens.

"Cavoc avenge me, my bloodline must be protected". David had spoken his last words; he was then engulfed in flames. The sun disappeared amongst dark clouds, the wild wind howled and then thunder and lightning bolts struck all around. The crowd quickly dispersed with the sounds of wild terror echoing all around. Mabus for the first time felt fear; he rushed to the safety of his study and then quickly bolted the door behind him. Darkness engulfed London. Mabus could hear the cries of frightened people as the mass panic continued. Mabus lit several candles and then to his absolute horror, Cavoc appeared from the shadows followed by five large beasts, which materialised with red glowing eyes. The creatures where snapping and snarling with razor sharp fangs.

Mabus looked all around with trembling hands paralysed with fear.

Cavoc looked into the eyes of Mabus and spoke, "You have made me so angry, look at my beasts they have not eaten for five moons they will reap your flesh".

Mabus begged for forgiveness. "Please Cavoc have mercy on me, I needed a war chest ready for my master he is to be reborn in the nineteenth century and he will wage war on the world and once more persecute the Jews".

"I know of Hisler or Hitler what ever his surname is, my friend Nostradamus believes his surname is to be Hisler. His book of perditions is now finished and in the nineteenth century man will read this book and hopefully put an end to your master".

"By the way your evil henchman Quino, who inflicted so much pain on my friend is being dealt with as we speak his beloved rats feed upon his flesh. How could anyone be so cold and corrupt. In the future this will not be tolerated, mankind will unite against such darkness and decay. I warned David not to return to this island of evil, you tricked him into coming here and then executed him and you then swore to destroy his bloodline, which was your fatal error. I cannot allow that to happen. We both worship different numbers, for you it is the three sixes. In the year of three sixes London will suffer the same fate as David; it will burn. It took your Queen Bloody Mary three minutes to sign David's death warrant, some might say she was mislead by your evil for this reason. I will give her three years; she will die without any true catholic bloodline.

"The peasants that watched will go hungry, their crops will fail. Now to you, the beasts moved closer and closer either side of Mabus. He shivered through his frame and then without warning the beasts pounced. He struggled, but to no avail as the beasts ripped him into little pieces with such savage ferocity. When the beasts had finished with the kill Cavoc and his beasts disappeared as they arrived back to the fifth dimension".

Santo finished his story back in the twentieth century, he rubbed his eyes and spoke, "That concludes the story

of David Burns, his son made sure the bloodline continued and much later the first five competed in the fifth
dimension to uphold the balance between good and evil.

I have now said all that needs to be said. Floyd shall
go first. The five sat around the table completely lost in
a hypnotic state. Santo looked to the first set of cards,
the place of battle, he picked up the first one. Santo
turned the card over and he gazed at a picture of a field.
He then looked to Floyd watching as he disappeared to
the Fifth dimension.

Floyd soon arrived he slowly opened his eyes and
inhaled the fresh air as he scanned all around. In the
distance he could see a dense dark forest, he looked
down to his feet he was standing on lush green grass, he
then raised his head and gazed up to the sky it was
cloudy and overcast.

The next card was dealt, a weapon a light appeared
in front of him, it slowly disappeared and then to his
amazement a golden spear appeared before his eyes. He
hesitated and then stepped forward bending over to
pick up the golden spear. He held it in his hand, it was
cold and heavy.

The third card was dealt; foe. All of a sudden
Floyd jumped as he heard a loud cry in the distance. He
gazed at the edge of the forest; a giant figure appeared
it began to move towards Floyd. The giant figure
moved closer and close.

The next card was dealt; help. A fairy appeared
before Floyd's eyes. He stood mesmerised by the sight

of the winged radiant angelic fairy. She wore clothes of green and red, eyes of emerald and long flowing golden locks. In a low-pitched voice she spoke, "I am here to be of assistance, in defeating your foe".

She then turned looking at the giant first, then she looked up at the overcast sky.

She began to talk in a strange dialect as though she was casting a spell; her sparkling wings began to move faster and faster. Floyd in a state of panic spoke, "What on earth is it?"

The fairy looked to Floyd putting on a brave face, "It is but a Troll, they are large cumbersome and of very low intelligence. In your hand is a Troll spear, on its tip is a poison, which will kill the Troll. As a back up I have prayed to the sun god, if the sun appears the Troll will turn to stone. But it could take a little while, we must keep the Troll preoccupied do you understand".

Floyd looked to the fairy, the plan seemed fool proof and he slowly began to gain confidence, forcing a smile he nodded his head they then looked to the Troll. He was now very close; the ground shook under his weight. Floyd gazed in disbelief the Troll was eight or nine feet in height. The Troll came to a halt puffing and panting, it then wiped the sweat from its brow and the Troll smiled then spoke in a deep voice, 'You smell good. I could smell you from several miles away; you must be my fast food delivery. I see you have come prepared is that a tooth pick?"

The Troll laughed out loud then turned his attention to the fairy, "Ah Tinkerbell how can you be of any help this is no fairytale?"

The fairy looked confused, she gazed into his big round bloodshot eyes; he had such a hideous appearance a huge nose and large yellow teeth she then spoke. "This is so strange you are not like other Trolls why are you not dim?"

Witted The Troll roared around with laughter.

"Hum, Hum, I smell the blood of a human you ain't got much meat on you but you will have to do as I haven't eaten in a week or two. A Troll saying poetry, I am different from the rest do you know any poetry little man?"

Floyd looked up at the Trolls huge biceps and razor sharp claws, he took a deep breath and recited a poem he had just made up, "Yes I am little, but your not going to eat me Mr Smelly, I will I shall throw my spear and your legs will turn to jelly".

The Troll pulled a funny face then spoke, "My you insult me, do I really smell?" The Troll lifted his right arm into the air and sniffed underneath it, "Oh maybe your right. Oh maybe your right. I do smell a bit. Now back to tinkerbell, as I approached you cast a spell pleading for the sun god to cast its rays and turn me to stone. Who knows I might be running out of time".

He then looked to Floyd, "Little man, that spear I know it is dipped with Troll poison, it is time to play. I will stand back here".

The Troll took three steps back, "Now I will stand still, go ahead throw your spear, give it your best shot. I must be careful that spear could kill me. Do you see size isn't everything, but if you miss you better run faster than a cheetah otherwise I will catch you and eat you".

The fairy looked to Floyd and spoke, "Look at the concentration in the Trolls eyes, we have but one chance. I must break that concentration and you must seize the opportunity to destroy him".

The Troll stood waiting silent with his large eyes completely focused on Floyd, the fairy began to fly to the left hand side of the Troll.

She got closer and closer as Floyd raised the spear and took aim. The Troll took no notice of the fairy he waited until the fairy was in range and in a split second he suddenly leaped into the air swatting the fairy like a fly with his giant hand. The impact sent her to the ground; her lifeless body lay motionless beneath his feet. Floyd became angry and threw the golden spear with lightning reflexes. The Troll dodged the spear, it missed him by an inch and the spear landed in the ground behind him.

The Troll laughed out loud and shook his head. "My that was close," he laughed out once more then spoke in a very loud voice, "Hum Hum you better run, going to eat you up my little pup".

Floyd turned around and began to run as fast as he could faster and faster he ran across the field, but he never stood a chance the Troll soon caught up with him and the Troll swiped his giant hand across Floyd s head the blow knocked him off his feet. The final card was dealt; Floyd lay on the ground the huge blow had left him dead. The Troll grabbed hold of Floyd's legs and dragged away the carcass for consumption. The troll began to sprint and was back on safe ground before the sunset, the card dealt was eaten.

The next to player was Ilene she disappeared from her chair reappearing in the Fifth dimension, she found herself in the woods. It was dense and gloomy; she moved her feet and could hear the rustle of fallen leaves. The wind began to howl, she looked to the sky and could see ravens circling overhead.

Their screams began to echo all around, Ilene felt a chill run down her spine. In the distance she could see a pathway and quickly moved towards it. Ilene looked to her left, suddenly her senses were filled with the sweet scents of wild flowers. The next card was dealt, all of a sudden a silver Winchester rifle appeared before her eyes. Ilene moved swiftly towards it, she bent down and picked up the rifle as memories of her childhood came flooding back to her. Her father kept rifles and had taught her to shoot from an early age, the rifle was loaded with five silver bullets.

She then heard a hideous howl as darkness engulfed her every move. Her heart began to pound, the leaves danced all around at the mercy of the wind. Ilene gazed up at the full moon. She had a morbid fear of the dark, her mind became paralysed with fear as the beast continued to howl. She listened in total horror; she knew the card that had been dealt was a fowl creature of the night. She began to walk along the path; again and again she could hear the howl of the beast as if it was closing in on her. Ilene continued to walk along the path until the path came to an end.

She stopped for a minute and took a deep breath she thought about her next move and then decided to carry on. She moved forwards, the ground was damp and she moved slowly with the rifle raised high. All of a sudden the beast stopped howling, her eyes where filled with wild terror she carried on walking until her shoulder was caught on a naked claw like branch. She shivered through her fragile frame as the beast moved closer and closer, until she could see a pair of large circular red glowing eyes staring at her.

Ilene froze upon realising the sheer size of the beast as it reared up on its hind legs, the creature was seven feet in length and it began to snap and snarl with its razor sharp fangs. Ilene aimed her rifle with trembling hands; suddenly she was plunged into darkness due to an eclipse of the moon. Ilene became hysterical shouting out where is my help, the next card was dealt and help arrived in the shape of a bright ray of light. It appeared lighting up the surrounding area. The beast cried out it had lost its advantage, the beast moved closer ready to pounce. The light blinded its eyes. Ilene seized on her opportunity and began to open fire. Two shots in quick succession; the silver bullets penetrated its heart. Ilene stepped back as the beast reached out its hairy arm, mercy was not the order of the day. Ilene fired the remaining bullets and the beast then fell to the ground howling in agony. An almighty bang then complete silence, the silver bullets proved fatal, its death was instant.

Ilene dropped the rifle and mumbled a prayer of gratitude the final card dealt was alive. Ilene was then transported back to the twentieth century as the victor. Ilene arrived as she left, on a chair in a trance like state.

Vesta was next, the card was dealt and he slowly disappeared to the fifth dimension. The place was a cliff. He found himself standing on a walkway built into a steep cliff, no signs of life occurred in the surrounding area. Vesta opened his eyes and stepped forward, treading carefully as he was walking on loose rocks. He gazed across a valley he could see a dark forest in the distance.

The atmosphere was cold and damp. Vesta glanced up to the sky, he could see masses of dark clouds and he carried on walking. A sense of doom engulfed his every move. Vesta drew a deep breath, all he could hear was the wailing wind and he felt a chill run down his spine. The second card was dealt, all of a sudden a large wooden stake appeared in front of him. Vesta hesitated and then cautiously moved forward and picked up the wooden stake. His mind then began to play tricks on him. What manner of creature could he be possibly be up against using a wooden stake as a weapon.

Vesta could see a dark macabre figure moving rapidly towards him closer and closer, faster and faster, until he could see what he was up against. It was gruesome, a witch dressed in a black robe complete with a black pointed hat. Her eyes were as dead as the night; her face was full of warts and wrinkles, teeth of yellow and rotted to the bone, her nails sharp as razor blades. Vesta was repulsed at the sight of her he stood motionless with a grave expression of horror. The next card was dealt; help. An ancient Bible appeared in front of his feet, he hesitated and then bent down and picked up the Bible. The card Belinda had given him fell out of his pocket onto the ground. The Witch stood and gazed at the card she then started to laugh out loud, she then spoke with a sickening tone a voice of pure evil and wickedness. "Go on pick it up, you know you want to. Oh Belinda is a distant cousin who shares the same name as me such a bewitching name is it not? Think back to the taxi ride". A look of disbelief began to fill Vestas face.

"No need too fret young man she told me she was going to cook you a nice steak". The witch began to lick her malignant lips. "Guess its me that will be having some fresh meat, oh and what a good boy you are you have brought some wood for my fire".

Vesta looked into her dark sinister eyes in a state of confusion, he spoke back to her in a angry voice, "How can that be? She is beautiful, I look to you and all I see is an ugly old hag".

The Witch began to laugh, "Young man there are two sides to every coin. I have supernatural powers, one of my sisters died in the European witch-hunt. I now walk the blessed earth seeking revenge on all that enter my domain. In your hand I see you have an old book. Is that a Bible can you read Latin?" Vesta shook his head and then placed the stake inside his jacket, he then carefully opened up the ancient Bible. He had been taught Latin from an early age the pages turned by themselves to a prayer Vesta read it out. In a hurry the witch ground her yellow rotten teeth.

"Two can play that game", she then cast a spell. Seconds later the Bible was engulfed in flames. Vesta dropped the book and stepped back, his wailing choking screams echoed all around. He looked to his burnt hands and then began to shiver in agony. He took a deep breath lifting the stake out of the jacket, he knew he had to kill the witch or be killed.

He remembered the Lords prayer and then started to recite it. The witch laughed. "Yes that's a good boy, pray to your maker, whoever that may be. Oh did I tell you as I am a witch I have powers to predict the future? I am afraid you are about to fall from a great height". The witch drew closer with an expression of diabolical evil.

Vesta moved forward with the razor sharp stake at the ready. The witch jumped into the air and onto Vesta he bravery fought back thrusting the stake into the witch's side. She let off a shriek so horrid the piecing sound echoed all around causing rocks to fall. The Witch grabbed Vesta by the throat, her sharp nails ripped into his larynx. Blood poured from the wound as tears came to his eyes, he then seemed to gain additional strength throwing himself off the cliff he kept tight hold of the witch. She fell also, as they both plunged one hundred and fifty feet the card had been dealt he fell to his death surrounded by stone.

It was now the turn of Edris, she disappeared from her seat slowly arriving in the fifth dimension. She felt the warm soft sand beneath her feet she then shielded her eyes from the blazing sun as it beat down on her with an unearthly radiance. Edris took a deep breath and slowly moved forward, she gazed all around. The card that was dealt; Arena. Edris was to do battle in an ancient circular Arena surrounded by several giant marble statues of Greek Gods. The second card was dealt and all of a sudden a sword appeared before her. She bent down and picked it up from the warm soft sand.

The sword was made of gold and silver. Keeping tight hold of the sword, she lifted it above her head then began to wave it around. She felt as though she was being watched. A strong smell of sulphur and then a demonic laugh. Edris turned to her left and saw a spine chilling sight with deep red skin, horns and hoofed feet. She gazed into its bright yellow snake eyes. The card had been dealt; the foe, that stood before her was the Devil himself.

The Devil smiled and then began to speak in a deep confident voice. "Hello Edris, your looking rather pale. Welcome to my place, it is but a haven for evil. You are an unfortunate soul, you are up against the ultimate evil. Underneath this arena I have my own little place I call it hell, it's full of lost souls later on I shall take you there, but first I must kill you.

"Cavoc informed me that your world will end soon. I feel so guilty that I will play no part in its destruction. The balance within the fifth dimension would be broken; a war between good and evil would commence. Cavoc will try to avoid this and will be looking for a solution to this problem. A dear friend of mine tried to pull it off in the nineteenth century, his was Dogma unfortunately mankind united and defeated him. I see you have the sword of Judah, it is so powerful it could quite possibly destroy me". Edris silently raised the sword the Devil smiled you look me up and down, "Yet you say nothing".

"Yes I am red, symbolizing both the fires of hell and the blood of humanity. You gaze into my demonic eyes, say something, your silence mocks me". Edris took a deep breath, the next card was dealt: a bright light and then an angel appeared next to Edris. The Devil laughed out loud then spoke, "Is that it? Many poor souls have perished here before me. I have never met my match and then I am sent you, how pitiful how unfortunate for you".

Edris carried on ignoring the Devil and gazed upon the angel who was so beautiful. She wore a pure white robe and had feathered wings, her radiant glow was truly mesmerising. Edris forced a smile and began to speak quietly. Her voice was filled with fear. "You must be here to help me defeat the Devil".

The angel blinked and then spoke ever so softly, "My poor child this is a dangerous situation, defeating the Devil wont be easy".

The Devil began to laugh out loud he then dropped to his knees, "I yield to your mercy. I will place my hands upon my head, go on give it your best shot after all you will need the luck of the Devil to defeat me".

The angel looked to Edris and began to whisper, "He is the great deceiver, look at the concentration in his evil eyes. I will divert him whilst you strike him with the sword of Judah".

The angel flew to the right of the Devil hovering closer and closer the Devil laughed.

"Oh you are so beautiful my angel, let me blow you a little kiss".

The Devil gazed at the angel; he placed his hand over his mouth and then blew her a kiss that ignited into flames. The angel's right wing was engulfed in flames and she cried out in pain. The Devil with lightning speed jumped into the air grabbing hold of the angels left wing, he then without mercy spun her around before he released his grip sending her spinning across the arena, she landed in a heap.

Edris stood frozen gazing at the lifeless body of the angel. The Devil blinked and the angel was once more engulfed in flames. Edris fell to her knees gripped by a hot flush panic. The Devil stood shaking his head he then spoke with rage in his voice, "There is nothing I despise more than a coward, get to your feet and put up a fight. I will give you a choice you fight and I will give you a quick and painless death, if not you will suffer pain beyond your imagination".

Edris stood back up, she knew she had to fight, so she drew a deep breath and spoke. "Good will conquer over evil on this day I shall defeat you".

The Devil laughed, "Good that the spirit, come closer little girl".

Edris moped the sweat from her forehead and then crept nervously forward towards the Devil, she moved closer and closer with the sword held high, the blade shone in the midday sun. Edris gritted her teeth summoning up courage, she lunged forward; the tip of the sword just missing the Devil she swung the sword bravely again and again to no avail.

The Devil moved with supernatural speed, he knocked the sword from her hand knocking her over onto the golden sand. He then picked her up and hurled her across the arena where she landed in a heap. Edris slowly got to her feet her body was aching all over; she knew her only chance was to escape. She took a deep breath then began to run across the arena, faster and faster she ran until she hit an invisible force field. She fell back onto the warm soft sand, she was left stunned for a couple of minutes as she closed her eyes then opened them slowly. The Devil stood over her he snarled then laughed as he spoke, "I am sorry but there is no escape, you put on such a pitiful display, go on take another deep breath it shall be your last".

Edris lay in the sand sweating furiously, the Devils grin of malice sent a shiver through her tiny frame her mind was paralysed by fear. The Devil picked her up once more she struggled but he was so powerful, he then snapped her neck and hurled her across the arena the card dealt was death.

The last of the five Steve was next, the card was dealt; he slowly disappeared from his seat and found himself standing in a swamp. Steve opened his eyes and gazed all around he could almost taste the damp smell, he then looked to his feet they where submerged in five inches of mud and slime. He started to walk; each step producing a sucking sound. He moved to the left to avoid a cloud of gnats, he staggered and inhaled a mouth full of swamp gas and he then began to cough out loud, the stench was unbearable.

The next card was dealt, all of a sudden a knife appeared in front of his eyes. The knife was embedded into a Cyprus tree. Steve waded over to the tree. He pulled the knife out of the tree and he gazed at its ivory handle and its silver razor sharp blade.

Steve listened to the sounds of the swamp; he could hear the mating calls of the frogs. He then gazed up to the moon as it lit up the swamp with a supernatural glow.

Steve then heard a hissing sound, he quickly turned around to his shock and complete horror he saw a monstrous snake rising out of the swamp, it had bright yellow skin patterns and large fangs. The next card was dealt; all of a sudden a white glowing light and then a man appeared. He was old, dressed in a brown robe. Steve gazed at his long white beard with great haste he spoke to Steve.

"My name is saint Aaron. I have come here to be of some assistance, listen to me; act very quickly the snake has but one weakness. Its eyes you must attack its eyes, with your knife".

Steve nodded his head and then concentrated on the snake as it moved closer and closer. Steve took a deep breath he then heard a voice from behind him. "Courage my son, have courage".

Suddenly with great speed the snake attacked, its mighty fangs sank into Steve's right shoulder. He fell backwards into the swamp the back of his head was submersed in the rancid water of the swamp, with all his strength he pushed his body back up, the snake released its grip and blood poured from the wound as Steve cried out in agony.

He then managed to get to his feet awaiting the next attack from the giant snake; Steve began to cough out loud as the snake resumed its attack. The snake looped its powerful body around Steve squeezing him with a vice like grip. Steve was a born fighter and began to wrestle the snake he then plunged the knife into the snakes eye.

Steve was finding it hard to breath as the snake continued with its slow suffocation, he cried out in pain. He then gained a new lease of life and he fought with great frenzy; repeatedly stabbing the snake again and again until the monster knew it was beaten and it released its grip. As Steve continued his onslaught like a man possessed, he thrust the razor sharp knife penetrating deep into the snakes hard scaly plates, until it fell from his arms back into the swamp with an almighty splash. It quickly sank to the bottom of the swamp.

Steve looked to his shoulder and arm, blood poured from his wounds, the knife slipped from his hand he then turned and looked to the saint. Steve was shaken and dazed and almost breathless with fatigue. His eyelids flickered spasmodically as he shouted. "What now, what now?"

His eyes were wild with terror he gazed at the saint with a fixed expression. The saint stood motionless; he then spoke, "You fought bravely my son but the final card has been dealt it is the blood card your fate has been sealed".

Steve shook his head in disbelief he then moved to a piece of dry land that was not submerged by the swamp, he fell to his knees and prayed for a miracle the saint suddenly appeared before him. He lit up with a luminous glare and began to speak ever so softly, "My God you deserve another chance my son, you have a brave heart. I shall seek the help you need".

And then with a blink of an eye had disappeared to the twentieth century. The saint appeared before Santo and Ilene. He glanced at Ilene then turned to Santo and spoke with an edge of coldness, "Santo you must help Steve he has fought so bravely he needs a nurse to ease his suffering".

Ilene felt a cold chill run down her spine. Santo looked into her eyes and spoke with a shade of impatience in his voice, "Come on Ilene, Steve needs you. Time is of the essence".

Ilene stood confused; she then agreed to help, nodding her head. Before she could speak the saint had raised his arms and they both materialized next to where Steve sat. Ilene looked to Steve blood pouring from a wound to his shoulder, she then turned to the saint, "What I am to do I have no bandages?"

The saint smiled, "You have immense compassion in your eyes, all you have to do is place your hand on his wound and he will be healed". Steve looked to Ilene.

He began to shake, his bottom lip he trembled as he spoke, "Please end my pain and suffering Ilene".

Tears trickled down her cheeks, she took a deep breath. Then moved forward placing her hand on Steve wound. The saint raised his arms whispering a sacred prayer and Steve was completely healed and on his way back to the twentieth century. Ilene had unwillingly traded places with Steve; she lay on the ground a feeling of repulsion that she had been deceived. Shivering in agony her choking screams echoed all around the swamp. Steve arrived back in the twentieth century, he stood next to Santo in a bewildered and confused state, he again looked to his shoulder; no pain, no wound. He was completely healed.

Condescending Santo smiled. "Good Steve your victory has prevailed. I know it was a cruel victory, but what is done is done you cannot return. You my son shall have plenty of time to grieve over your fallen Conrad".

Steve looked to Santo in confusion he felt a strange tingling sensation he then drew a deep breath and said, "Where is Ilene, what has happened to her".

Santo shook his head, he then looked to Steve with fixed eyes, "I fear what I am about to say will displease you".

Ilene placed her hand on your shoulder and took your place, she now sits in the swamp bleeding to death in agony".

Steve closed his eyes, suddenly his anger rose. "God damn you," he cried. "There must be something we can do help her".

Santo shook his head an anxious silence then Santo spoke out.

"Steve there could be only one winner, it was you or Ilene. Steve began to calm down he knew Santo words where true".

Steve I was once the victor as you are now, you are the last you shall inherit all the wealth of the five fives.

Author's note

I have always enjoyed writing and started off with poetry, I became a member of the poetry society. I completed over five hundred poems on a variety of subjects. I then became a member of the Guild of International Song Writers and Composers.

I have always been a prolific writer and have a vast collection of poems and short stories. My completed poems have been published in *The Standard* newspaper for the last twenty years. I often had people contacting me telling me how much they enjoyed my poems. Some of the poems I wrote to my total amazement predicted future events. I believe we all have a degree of physic potential that lies dormant until it is activated.

I have experienced such potential over the past years. I remember having a vision of a helicopter crashing. I then turned on the television to find it Breaking News. Another example is when I think of someone I haven't heard of for a long time and minutes later they contact me. I often listen to music and on lots of occasions I have thought of a song I haven't heard of for a long time, I would turn the radio on and the song will be playing or about to be played.

I remember many years ago riding to work on a bicycle with a friend. I told him I had a vision about being crushed by steel, after work we were riding home when a heavy goods vehicle loaded with steel pulled out in front of us, the driver hit his breaks just missing us. My story *The Five Fives* came to me in a series of visions, unlocking the mysteries that have haunted mankind through out the centuries.

I believe in the power of numerology, numbers compose the very foundation of reality; throughout the centuries people have believed it is possible to predict the future. I have studied numerology for many years, it is based on the belief numbers are not solid objects but vibrations and energies that move. These vibrations influence our lives with either the dark shadow side negative experiences; separation, or light positive experiences; connection. Your destiny can be determined using numerology, Philosopher Pythagoras studied numerology. He believed, as I do, numbers are the essence of life.

I was born in October my collective year, which shows my qualities are bringing wisdom to the world. My personal year table is the number five which represents communication each number contains emotional, mental, physical and spiritual dimensions. This is why numerology is such an amazing representation of life.

The basis of numerology is that we are influenced by our birth name and our birthdate. The numbers five and eight have influenced me throughout my life. An example of this is in two thousand and fourteen I had two accidents. I added the date and the month together and came up with the numbers five and eight. Throughout my life I have lived at number five or eight. I believe when these numbers clash my luck turns bad, as together these numbers add up to thirteen. I mentioned earlier about my poems, some of which predicted future events. I remember gazing at the front cover of a newspaper at the sad face of Princess Diana.

I put pen to paper and wrote a poem about the Princess in the summer of nineteen ninety-seven recalling the ending of the poem.

Life goes fast when you are so harassed,
you sealed your fate when you made that date,
don't cry Di it was meant to be.

Two months later she went on a date with Dodi and they were harassed by the paparazzi and they both was died under tragic circumstances. Another strange thing that happened to me when I was moving autographed pictures in my barroom in the summer of two thousand and three. I have got over a dozen pictures, I placed them on the floor, all of a sudden I noticed a large fly sitting on the face of Charles Bronson.

I chased the fly away only for it to return to the same spot later. I found out Charles Bronson had died. In two thousand and twelve I sat watching the movie *The Bodyguard* later on I put an episode of a eighties series called *Thiller,* the episode I put on was about a killer who would meet women and drown them in their bath tubs. Later on I heard the news about Whitney Huston. In the past I have had dreams about celebrities and then the following morning I have turned on the news to find out they had passed away. I have read prediction is very difficult especially about the future; I once worked at a large warehouse that employed hundreds. The canteen staff started off a weekly raffle, each week I would buy one strip of five tickets. I won nine weeks on the run, prizes such as a £100 hamper. The bizarre thing was I would write on the back of the ticket the winning ticket before the draw and that ticket would win the prize.

I visited a local social club, which was full of people buying raffle tickets. I bought my usual strip of tickets and the draw took place, I won the first prize and was then invited to pick out the next ticket, I won again. Someone else picked out the third and fourth tickets. I remember the faces around the club as I had won all four prizes with my five tickets. I became so confident believing I just couldn't lose. A friend asked me to go out for a drink and I agreed, we went out to a local pub, inside the pub they were selling raffle tickets for a cash prize. I informed my friend that I would buy some tickets and later we should return and I would give him half of the money. We returned later as usual I wasn't disappointed I kept my word and gave my friend half the money.

On another occasion a friend told me that he had never won anything in his life, we entered a pub selling raffle tickets for a meat hamper. I informed my friend that if he were to go up and buy a ticket, that he would win the hamper. He agreed and to his total amazement he won for the first time in his life.

I expected to win every time I bought a raffle ticket. I remember entering a pub buying some raffle tickets. I never won first prize, so I ripped up the tickets in disbelief. I had to put the ticket back together as it was unknown to me that there was a second prize, I had a bizarre winning streak which continued for many years. Then I started filling in a pools coupon I started off eight from eleven, weeks later I changed to eight from ten, what a mistake I had accidently put an extra cross on the winning line that would have won a small fortune.

The company in question sent me a cheque for a sum in good faith, I remember thinking to myself perhaps I wasn't destined to win such a large sum of money. My lucky and unlucky numbers have always been five and eight these two numbers have always played a part in my life. Every week I used the same two numbers and the one week I didn't use them I found out I had all the winning numbers except five and eight. I believe eventually I will win picking out the correct winning numbers. I remember visiting the supermarket several times and guessing the correct price of the shopping in the trolley without adding it up, I informed the lady on the till how much the bill would be before she started to scan them and I was correct. She looked at me and said,

"I bet you couldn't do that again". I informed her that I had already guessed the correct price of my shopping on several occasions.

I was driving to the town centre I had a vision of a woman stepping out onto the road in front of my car. I returned home and began to write down about my vision. Every day I wrote short stories. I was once in bed after working a night shift, I could see characters and a story unfolding. I knew that if I didn't write the story onto paper I would not be able to sleep, I sat up and then picked up a pen and a large note pad. I began writing at a prolific pace. I found myself in a trance like state. I wrote nonstop for over one hour and when the story was completed, I just looked at the amount of pages in amazement.

I had written a complete short story entitled *Wits About*. It was a truly amazing horror story. I remember competing in the Great North Run I had a vision of a young man wanting to compete in the London Marathon, his father was a gangster controlling the north of England. He eventually grants his son permission to run in the London marathon as long as he took a trusted bodyguard. Things go wrong in the south and then all hell breaks out between the north and south, this is probably the best gangster story ever written, full of twists and gang warfare.

As with all the short stories I have written I can picture the characters as though I was watching a movie. The ideas I had for short stories are all original. I was the most prolific in the year two thousand and three a short story entitled: *The judgement Angels and Demons.*

And then a science fiction story several years later I bought a DVD called *The Knowing.* I watched this movie in total disbelief; the story was about a professor John predicting future disasters. The short story I had written was very similar to this movie, which I had written in two thousand and three. The main character in my story was a professor John. I continued to write more and more stories only on one occasion have I stopped writing half way through a short story, as it was the most frightening story.

I mentioned earlier I could see all of the characters and the surrounding as if I was on a film set. The story was about the supernatural. Imagine being on the film set of the most frightening film ever made, this is the reason I stopped writing. I sent off ideas to the BBC and various publishers. I believe this was a mistake on my behalf. I remember thinking I have over six hundred short stories I just wanted feedback. One of the first stories I ever wrote just after the millennium was entitled *The Five Fives.* I had a vision of David Burns travelling to the fifth dimension and meeting Cavoc. Later I decided to write Nostradamus into my story.

Every time I wrote fiction later researching and finding it to be fact, for instance I wrote Nostradamus was in Montpellier on a certain date and John Dee in Paris on another date, to my amazement fiction turned to fact

I also wrote the world would end in the year two thousand and twenty-five, several years later I researched Nostradamus and found out he wrote his predictions, until the year two thousand and twenty-five. Some people have questioned this believing it to be a sign the world will end on this date. One of the endings was a large comet. I was shocked to find out a giant comet named Swift will just miss earth in the year twenty twenty-five.

I finished the *Five Fives* story whilst cruising around the Caribbean. In the same year I went on holiday to Ibiza, the night-time entertainment at the hotel was poor, my son said to me how about playing cards. I hadn't played for a while and eventually we ran out of games to play. He then said I'll shuffle the pack and you have to pick out the correct card. I had never performed any card tricks. He asked me to pick the ten of hearts. To his amazement I picked out the correct card and then the ten of diamonds again and again! I picked out whatever card he said.

My daughter had made friends with a group of teenagers they all looked like characters out of the *Harry Potter* movie, one in particular informed me of that he could perform magic tricks, my son said that he wanted three kings. I picked each of the kings one after another; I soon had an audience around me. The *Harry Potter* look alike picked up the deck and shuffled it, he then said I want you to pick out the queen of spades. I concentrated on the deck of cards and then to everyone's amazement I picked out the correct card, his words were, "My God how did you do that?"

The rest of the audience made similar comments. I cannot explain how I picked out all the correct cards but there were plenty of witnesses.

All of this happened in the year two thousand and thirteen. I mentioned earlier about numbers governing our lives. My son was walking along the pavement when a car accidently mounted the pavement knocking him down in bizarre circumstances, the person lived at number eight and their Christian and surname were five letters long.

I was involved in an accident myself, the person also lived at number eight and his Christian and surname were both five letters long. In the same year my father tragically died on the eighth of December, these two numbers have always played a part in my life, lucky or unlucky. I have written just a few examples of how these numbers have affected me. I have written the follow up to *The Five Fives* it is entitled *David* and just like *The Five Fives* the story is truly amazing!

Lightning Source UK Ltd.
Milton Keynes UK
UKOW04f1929130315

247870UK00001B/20/P